Yuletide Yarns

©2002, Mike McCarthy & Alice Lannon, eds.

Le Conseil des Arts | The Canada Council
du Canada | for the Arts

We acknowledge the support of The Canada Council for the Arts for our publishing program.

We acknowledge the financial support of the Government of Canada through the Book Publishing Industry Development Program (BPIDP) for our publishing program.

Cover Art: Joanne Snook-Hann
Cover Design: Joanne Snook-Hann & Todd Manning
∞ Printed on acid-free paper

Published by
CREATIVE PUBLISHERS
an imprint of CREATIVE BOOK PUBLISHING
a division of Creative Printers and Publishers Limited
an Opti-Press Inc. associated company
P.O. Box 8660, St. John's, Newfoundland A1B 3T7

First Edition
Typeset in 11.5 point Book Antiqua

Printed in Canada by:
ROBINSON-BLACKMORE PRINTING & PUBLISHING

National Library of Canada Cataloguing in Publication

Yuletide yarns : stories of Newfoundland and Labrador Christmases gone by / Mike McCarthy & Alice Lannon, editors.

Includes bibliographical references.
ISBN 1-894294-50-5

1. Christmas--Newfoundland and Labrador. 2. Newfoundland and Labrador--Social life and customs. I. McCarthy, Michael J., 1932- II. Lannon, Alice, 1927-

GT4987.15.Y84 2002   394.2663'09718   C2002-904185-6

Yuletide Yarns

Stories of Newfoundland and Labrador Christmases Gone By

Mike McCarthy
&
Alice Lannon, eds.

St. John's, Newfoundland
2002

To the memory of our deceased parents, Thomas and Julia McCarthy and all the Newfoundland writers who have helped preserve the memory of the old time Christmas customs of Newfoundland and Labrador and passed them on to the next generation.

TABLE OF CONTENTS

SECTION THREE – CHRISTMAS MEMORIES OF NEWFOUNDLAND AND LABRADOR

SECTION FOUR – NEWFOUNDLAND AND LABRADOR CHRISTMAS TRAGEDIES

Acknowledgements

Special thanks to:

- Mona Cram
- Annie Follett
- Frank Galgay
- The late Frank Graham
- Brenda Humby
- Yvonne Humby
- David Leamon and staff of the Newfoundland Reference Library
- Beth and Steve Mandville
- Anna McCarthy
- Kit McGrath
- Paddy O'Reilly
- Ann Pennell
- Captain Joe Prim
- Staff of the Provincial Archives

Foreword

Christmas has always been a season of celebration in Newfoundland and Labrador. As early as 1754, the court records show that Christmas was celebrated in Bay Bulls with house visitations and plenty of flip, a strong mixture of rum and spruce beer. There was dancing and house visitations and the fetching home of the man of the house for supper.

In 1770, Captain George Cartwright described the Christmas celebration on his trading post at Cartwright on the Labrador coast. The festivities began with building up a huge fire in the crew's house, and the firing of a gun to mark the beginning of Christmas. Then each man present drank a dram of rum, gave three cheers and got down to the serious business of drinking. There were arguments and fights, but it seems a good time was had by all.

The old Christmas customs of England, Ireland, Scotland and France were brought over by the early settlers and blended over the years into a unique Newfoundland style of celebration. In the communities along our six thousand miles of coastline people still celebrate many of the old customs, like firing off guns, having "sweet bread" and plum pudding and going out in the mummers or jannies and getting home for Christmas is still important to nearly every Newfoundlander.

To emphasis the importance of a Newfoundlander getting home for Christmas, there is a story told about a gentleman who died and arrived at the pearly gates on Christmas Eve. He was waiting for St. Peter to open the gate to admit him, when a group of men, women and children suddenly rushed out and quickly disappeared. At that moment St. Peter told the man to enter. However, the man suddenly had doubts and said to St. Peter, "Before I enter, I want to know why those people just rushed out of there?" "Oh that crowd," answered St. Peter, "that's just the Newfoundlanders going home for Christmas, they do it every year."

Christmas Customs of

Newfoundland and Labrador

Going Out in the Mummers or Jannies

by Alice Lannon & Mike McCarthy

The custom of going out in the mummers or darbies or jannies came to Newfoundland from both England and Ireland, and is perhaps the oldest Christmas custom. Although now greatly reduced, it is still carried on in our province. In fact, the first mummers or Morris dancers were brought to Newfoundland by Sir Humphrey Gilbert on his ill-fated voyage of 1583. In most places on the Avalon Peninsula there were mummers, but at the Head of Conception Bay and at St. Mary's Bay they were called darbies. However, on the West Coast of Newfoundland and the Great Northern Peninsula the term jannies was used. In some places such as Harbour Grace they were called both mummers and jannies.

Originally there were two types of mummers in Newfoundland, the "fools" and the "mummers." In an article in the *Evening Telegram's* Christmas Number for 1885, William Whittle, who had left St. John's in 1847 for Boston, described the antics of one of the "fools" when he was a young boy.

> I remember some years ago, just about Christmas time, one of my brothers, who was quite a genius in that line, making a full-rigged brig, and giving it to a person who was to be a "fool" on New Year's Day,

to be used in decoration of his cap, with the understanding the brig was to be mine at the end of the day. Well, bright and early on New Year's morning I presented myself at the door of the "fool" fully two hours before the hour came for him to dress. Finally out he came, "dressed to kill" or "mash" as the saying goes now. His milk-white shirt sleeves were literally covered with ribbons. His pantaloons were of the heaviest broadcloth; and his cap surmounted with my coveted prize—the full-rigged brig. Down Limekiln Hill he went with the fleetness of a deer—and there was method in this as he was anxious that few should know where he emerged from. And down I went after him. Up Playhouse Hill he ran until his eye lit on someone who like himself was swift afoot. Then commenced the chase. Up lanes, across lots, down lanes, in and out of the crowd, until the person chased sought shelter in some hallway. Yet his haven was not secure, for with his shoulder against the door, the "fool" was determined that it should yield. Then came a critical moment, for I saw an impending danger to the spars of the brig, then came the warning cry "stoop! stoop!" He obeys the command, the door is forced open, the victim secured, a few friendly taps on the legs and they shake hands and walk out together. From Playhouse Hill to the Mall, from the Mall to the Tickle, many times that day did I follow that fool. Wherever the crowd was greatest, there I was, like Mr. Fezziwig in Dickens' *Christmas Carol* in their midst. At last, late at night, when the "fool" weary, tired, all played out, sought his home, I was made the happy owner of the full-rigged brig.

"Munn" Carter, I remember was always a conspicuous "fool" and one who could handle himself well, for Munn was a fellow whom every would-be boxer did not want to tackle. Dave Foley was always the owner of a stylish rig, while his friend, Mosey Murphy, appeared, I think as an "owen-shook." The "owen-shook" was always a terror to encounter, for he was rarely merciful to anyone who made him draw upon his wind, and woe to the man who disputed his right of giving a sound castigation for the trouble incurred.

Reverend Philip Tocque, a native of Carbonear, described the mummers of his youth, which would be around 1820. He said there were two classes of mummers; those who went out by night and those who went out by day. The male "day mummers" would have white shirts trimmed with ribbons over their clothes and wore fancy hats. Each man had a partner—a man dressed in women's clothes. The "night mummers" were dressed in the most grotesque costumes with horns and hobby horses over their heads. They also carried small bags of flour which they threw over their followers. The most feared night mummer was the "owen-shook" who showed no mercy to anyone he might encounter.

Sir Richard Bonnycastle described the fools in 1842. They dressed in grotesque masks with highly decorated huge paper cocked hats. They went in groups as each fool had several attendants to serve his wants. Young fishermen represented the ladies and did not wear masks but instead painted their faces. The leaders of the fools carried whips and bladders filled with pebbles and used these to belabour the spectators to amuse themselves. Some people called the fools "Oonchucks" which simply meant men in women's clothing.

The fools in St. John's began their revels with a visit to Government House and then went on to other houses. They expected a present of money to finance a ball on

Old Christmas Day. A.J. Parsons, a prominent Newfoundland journalist, described the "Hobby Horse" of his youth in an article in the December 1917 issue of *Holly Leaves.*

A weird figure bearing the head of a horse, nodding and gesticulating wildly to his companions, who were attired in all kinds of fantastic dress paraded Water Street and halted at the foot of Market House Hill where now stands the new Court House. The oddly garbed figures meanwhile capering in amusing fashion around the hobby horse, as I found the centre figure was called, chasing people and striking them with whips at the ends of some of which were attached inflated bladders. Father Christmas was easily recognizable whilst St. George of Merrie England indulged in rough horseplay with his companions. All the characters wore masks, several of them were clad in feminine apparel, but it was easy to determine by their ungainly antics and loud meaningless talk, that they were all of the opposite sex.

There was also the "Mummers' Play" brought over from the old country and acted out with great vigour. In many a far flung Newfoundland community the classical heroes of Greece and Rome and great historical characters came to life again in the old lines memorized and given with great vigour by illiterate fisherman. One version of the play was brought to Port Kirwin by an old Irish teacher named William O'Neill, better known to his students as "Old Tack." This version of the Mummers' Play required fourteen men who each portrayed different characters. The play involved a dispute between two English aristocrats. Among the cast of characters were King William, Beelzebub, the knight, the knight's lady, the Doctor, the Doctor's lady and an old horse. Each character had a dialogue to perform. In Port Kirwin the play was repeated in a different house each night and was followed by a "scuff and a scoff." These mummers were all dressed in their Sunday best. Crepe paper rosettes were pinned to the jacket of the suit. The words and characters of the play usually differed from community to community, but the story line was very much the same. One of the antagonists was killed, but the doctor brought him back to life with his odd assorted magic potions.

Canon George Earle recalled that his father, who was born in 1886 at Change Islands in Notre Dame Bay, could remember as a boy seeing the Mummer's Play performed in that community. The play had been brought to the community by a teacher named Justinian Dowell around 1870. It too was a version of the Hero-Combat play.

Around 1850, a group of mummers performed the Mummer's Play of "St. George" at Government House for Governor Sir John Harvey. However, the mummers got caught up in the political turmoil that engulfed Conception Bay during the early elections that followed the granting of Responsible Government in 1855 and there were some incidents where the mummers or fools took advantage of their disguise to settle old scores. In fact, it was an assault on a man named Isaac Mercer in Bay Roberts on the evening of December 28th, 1861 that made mummering in Newfoundland illegal, unless the person or persons involved had a written license from a magistrate.

Mercer and his two brothers-in-law were coming out of the woods late in the evening, when six mummers set upon them with pickets and beat them to the ground.

Isaac Mercer was beaten so badly that he died the next day from the effects of the blows. The government offered a reward of 100 pounds for information leading to the identity of the attackers, but it was never claimed. On June 25, 1861, the House of Assembly passed an Act which prohibited any mummering unless the person or persons had a written licence from a magistrate or Justice of the Peace. The penalty for breaking this law was seven days in jail or a fine of twenty shillings.

While this law was enforced in St. John's, mummering still went on in the outports pretty much as before, and in fact continues right up to the present time in many communities. A visit from the mummers is announced by a loud knock on the door and a voice speaking in "mummer talk" asks the age old question, "Any mummers 'llowed in?" In recent years there has been an attempt to revive the practice of mummering in St. John's and other larger towns.

The Christmas Tree in Newfoundland Christmas Customs

by Mike McCarthy

Although the Christmas tree is a common symbol of Yuletide in most Newfoundland homes today, it is a comparatively recent Christmas custom as far as Newfoundland is concerned. The custom of having Christmas trees came from Germany and is very ancient. The people of Norway, Sweden and Denmark adopted this custom from the Germans and brought small trees into their homes at Christmastide.

The first recorded use of a Canadian evergreen as a Christmas tree occurred in 1781 in Sorel, Quebec. It was erected by Baron Friederick von Riedesel, a German national who decorated his Christmas tree with white candles. The next recorded Canadian Christmas tree was in Halifax in 1846. It was erected by a merchant named William Pryor. He set up the tree to please his German wife, and imported glass ornaments from Germany to decorate.

The first well known use of a Christmas tree in England was in 1841, when Prince Albert, the consort of Queen Victoria, had a Christmas tree set up at Windsor Castle and decorated it. This practice was quickly adopted by many English families.

The Hessian soldiers who served as British merce-naries in the American War of Independence in 1776, brought the Christmas tree tradition to the United

States. Later German immigrants spread this Christmas custom to many parts of that country.

In Newfoundland one of the first references to a Christmas tree comes from Harbour Breton on the Southwest coast of the island. In this community, on Holy Innocents' Day, December 28, 1867, the Anglican Rector, Reverend W. White and Mrs. White entertained the children of the Sunday school and day school of St. Bartholomew's church at the Rectory.

Photo courtesy of Mrs. Susan (White) Moulton

A 1956 Garnish Christmas Tree

Following evening prayers at 3 p.m. the children went to the Rectory and sat down to tea which had been prepared for them as a Christmas treat. However, the most fascinating object in the room was a beautiful

Christmas tree decorated with fruit, and from the tree each child at the tea party was given a piece of fruit.

However, despite its early introduction to Fortune Bay there were places like Terrenceville in the bay where the Christmas tree was still a novelty in the 1930s. In Labrador it was the Moravian Missionaries who introduced the Christmas tree to the native people of Labrador and by 1892 there was a Christmas tree in every home of the communities served by the Moravians. As well, a Moravian missionary named W.W. Perrett is credited with first introducing Father Christmas to the Labrador coast.

Dr. Grenfell and his nurses brought the Christmas tree to the inhabitants of Northern Newfoundland and it soon became a popular Christmas tradition all along that coast. At first the Christmas trees were set up at the hospital residence and the schools, but soon were being set up in individual homes. Again, the early Christmas trees in this area were decorated with apples and oranges which were given to visiting children. This was followed by decorations made of orange and apple papers and a homemade star cut from cardboard and covered with lead from a tea chest was placed at the top of the tree.

Writing about Christmas in St. John's in 1870, Dr. Louise Whiteway says that "the Christmas tree has not yet come into its own." However, on January 8, 1872, the St. John's *Times* gave the following report of a Christmas celebration in near-by Pouch Cove which included two Christmas trees:

> On Tuesday week the children of the Church and Board schools of Pouch Cove to the number of 150 were assembled by the Reverend R.M. Johnson and Mrs. Johnson to enjoy the festivities got up for Christmas and New Year season. The entertainment

commenced at 3 p.m. with a game of football in which everyone joined and enjoyed very much in spite of snow on the ground. At 4 p.m. they assembled in the day Sunday school room where two large Christmas trees were unveiled and the various articles which grew on the branches were distributed to the children.

As a finale to the entertainment, a number of sky rockets were set off which enlightened the children on their way home to bed.

John Maclay Byrne, a native of St. John's who lived in Boston makes no mention in his book — *The Path to Yesterday* — of Christmas trees in his description of a family Christmas in St. John's around 1890. However by 1892 it appears that some families had Christmas trees in that city, for in a poem published in *Christmas Bells* in that year, Ellen Carberry (who wrote under the pen name E.C.) makes reference to the children's toys being under the Christmas tree.

In 1906, the Salvation Army at Harbour Grace had a public Christmas tree and gifts from the tree were given to the poor. Reg Sparkes in his book, *The Winds Sigh Softly*, tells us that Christmas trees were in use in Jackson's Arm, White Bay, in the early nineteen hundreds. The Christmas tree was put up after supper on Christmas Eve and decorated with a few store-bought glass decorations and lots of homemade ones, including some made from wool and a few cut from tin. Apples were also hung from the tree to enhance its beauty.

In *Trail Wanderings*, Mrs. Queen Maloney writes that the first Christmas trees were introduced to the Bay Bulls area in 1920. The decorations on these Christmas trees were twists made from orange paper, and little twists of candy tied up in little bundles of lace from an old curtain. The star for the top of the tree was cut from cardboard and covered with lead from a tea chest.

In his book *On Sloping Ground*, Aubrey M. Tizzard states that when he was a young boy in Hillgrade, Twillingate District, in the late 1920s, no one in the community had Christmas trees in their homes. It wasn't until his older sister, Eleanor, returned from a spell in hospital a few years later that his family put up their first Christmas tree. There were community Christmas trees in such places as Beaumont and Lushes Bight in the early 1920s.

In Bonavista Bay, some communities had Christmas trees in the 1920s. A lady from Summerville remembers having a tree with store bought decorations in the 1920s. Only a few families had store-bought Christmas ornaments. The majority of people had to make do with their own homemade Christmas tree decorations.

In Placentia Bay, the custom of having a Christmas tree began as early as 1917 in some communities. In others it didn't catch on until the late 1930s. A former resident of Argentia in the days before the coming of the American Base, can remember seeing her first Christmas tree in that community in 1936. This Christmas tree was a great novelty and the family had decorated it with shining red apples. When a neighbouring child visited the house during Christmas they were given an apple from the tree as a present. However, in South East Placentia, the first Christmas tree was introduced around 1917 by Mrs. Lucy (St. George) Lannon. In Little Bonia, Placentia Bay, the custom of having a Christmas tree originated around the same time as at South East Placentia. The decorations, as in most other Newfoundland outport communities, were handmade.

In St. Leonard's, Placentia Bay, there was at least one house with a Christmas tree in 1917.

Writing about his memories of Christmas around 1920 in New Harbour, Trinity Bay, Ron Pollett in his book, *The Ocean at My Door,* makes no mention of Christmas trees in his community.

During the 1930s and 1940s, and especially after the arrival of the Americans in 1941, the custom of having a Christmas tree spread to most Newfoundland communities. Today it is an almost universal Christmas custom in most Newfoundland homes.

Hunting the Wren (1893)

by W. P.

In 1893 an article by an anonymous writer W.P. in the St. John's CHRISTMAS BELLS annual of that year described the origins of an old Irish Christmas custom called "Hunting the Wren." This custom has just about died out in Newfoundland, although in 1969, it was still carried on in some Newfoundland communities. (Editors)

W.P.'s Article

"Hunting the Wren" is a merry pastime with some of our boys on St. Stephen's Day, but few perhaps know the origin of the custom.

The wren was the Augur's favourite bird. The Druids represented him as the "King of the Birds" and even when our ancestors embraced Christianity it was considered unlucky to kill this bird.

> A Robin and a wren
> Are God Almighty's cock and hen.

And any one who killed either of these birds or destroyed their nests was said to be sure to break a bone or meet with some other dreadful misfortune. Hence the wren was surrounded by a great superstitious respect. This gave offence to the first Christian Missionaries to Britain and by their command they were hunted and killed on Christmas Day and also on the following day, St. Stephen's Day. The custom has reached to our day (1893) and place (Newfoundland).

Another Irish account records that at the last battle fought in the North of Ireland between the contending parties in the days of the Commonwealth at Glensuly in the County Donegal, that one of these parties would have been surprised sleeping were it not been for several wrens that just awakened them by dancing and pecking on the drum as the enemy was approaching, a story that reminds us of the saving of Rome by the cackling of geese. Whichever gave rise to this practice, we still have it in our midst.

On St. Stephen's Day the wren is carried about hung by the leg on a small bush "bedecked with ribbons gay" and a procession made by the boys from house to house who declared him to be the king of all birds and sang the following ditty:

The wren, the wren the King of all birds;
On St. Stephen's Day was caught in the firs,
And although he is little, his family is great,
So arise good lady and give us a treat.

And if you fill it of the small,
It will not do for our boys at all,
But if you fill it with the best,
We hope in heaven your soul will rest.

Oh Mr. _____ is a worthy man
And to his house we have brought our wren,
Sing holly, sing ivy, sing ivy, sing holly,
He'll give us a drop to drown melancholy.

A Glimpse of Christmas in the Olden Times

by P. K. Devine

The festive season of Christmas is a time when the mind goes back in either sad or glad retrospection to the days that are gone forever. I have always enjoyed each Christmas as a milestone marking the highway of the journey of life. At this time, memory is more active and more faithful than at other times as we look back over the past with mingled feelings of pleasure and sadness. Tennyson expresses the feeling of mankind when he says:

> They bring me sorrow touched with joy
> The merry bells of Yuletide.

Many a Christmas of the past stands out in vivid distinction and the remembrance of the scenes and faces now departed produce feelings too acute for expression in words. The old customs that marked the Yuletide of our youth have gone in the outport as well as the city. They exist now only in memory. No more shall we hear the volley of musketry fired from old sealing guns on Christmas Eve announcing the advent of the joyous season. Activated by the practical spirit of the age, the fisherman now keeps his powder to kill birds or seals. No more we see the fires of big birch logs glowing in the wide open fireplace with its cattrill and dog-irons. The stove is now set up in every kitchen for economy in using the supply of wood. No more do gangs of men repair to the forest at dawn on the morning of the twenty-fourth to select the biggest trees to cut them into Yule logs. The wood is now used for the more practical purpose of building boats and making "stannes" and "headings." The sand and sawdust swept into neat borders on the kitchen floor are superseded by painted canvas and the long settle and the arm chairs are replaced by the upholstered furniture and the dining room suite too frail for lusty fishermen to move about on. The general unhurried and relaxation of spirit among the people who assembled in the big hospitable kitchen is no longer witnessed.

Manners regarded as more polite and more civilized now prevail and the old spontaneity and indulgence in "quips" and jokes and jollity is now considered bad form. The tea meeting and the lantern show have taken their place and the cotillion and the reel are not indulged in anymore.

The mummers were the great institution in the Christmas Season in the olden days. The genuine mummers of forty years ago must not be confused with the ordinary and latter-day members of the cult who merely dressed or disguised themselves in fantastic costumes and went from house to house dancing and drinking. The real mummers were men of importance and to be in the caste was considered to be an honour equal to that of being a top-sawyer or master of a cod seine skiff. They represented the great heroes of history including St. George, Bonaparte, Alexander, Hector, St. Patrick, Wellington, etc. and each one stepped forward and recited his verses that recounted the brave deeds the hero had done. No wonder that a glamour of romance surrounds these good old timers in the minds of the older generation that revelled in them. They were truly the peaceful times when Christmas free from care and toil was kept up for twelve days.

"Bringing Home The Yule Log." Taken from *The Illustrated London News* Christmas Number, 1881. — 33. Drawn by A. Hunt, Engraved by R. Loudan.

Or is it that the haze of grief
Makes former gladness loom so great
The lowness of the present state
That seeks the past in this relief.
Or that the past will always win
Of glory from its being far
And o'er unto the perfect star
We saw not when we moved therein.

Without stopping to consider the right answer to the problem propounded by Tennyson, we find not the least doubt that our ancestors took more hearty enjoyment out of the festive season than we do today. They entered into the influence of the time unreservedly and with a zeal that left no time for regret when the season was over that they had not their best to celebrate it.

There was of course a good deal of hard drinking but the liquor was cheap and good. It was one of the customs of the time and when a text from Scripture on the subject was selected for the occasion it was found in St. Paul to Timothy where he advises taking "a little wine for the stomach's sake." Also that which says: "Wine maketh glad the heart of man." A prosperous fishery meant always a well-kept up Christmas and no deaths in December meant much dancing and much mummering. If one of the neighbours in the harbour happened to be very ill, all prayed fervently that he or she might not die until after the Twelfth Day, because if a death occurred it put a damper on the festivities and made it necessary that no dancing should be heard within sound of that house, and men did dance in those days. No mincing dances in fine slippers but "Round the House" evolutions, the heartiness and spontaneity of which left no room for the observer to doubt that the participants were enjoying themselves.

We should like to see the Historical Society making an effort to preserve an account of the Christmas celebrations in Newfoundland in the good old days. It would be of greater interest fifty years hence than now. It materially belongs to the history of the country and therefore should be collected and written down. The heroic plays held by the mummers would be most interesting and it is quite possible that there may be living some of the heroes of history who took part in the festivities.

Quaint Christmas Customs

by P. K. Devine

Nearly every civilized country in the world has its customs and superstitions peculiar to Christmas, and to this rule Newfoundland is no exception. Our forefathers brought their traditions with them, from England, Ireland and Scotland, and they are, though gradually dwindling away, still handed down to their descendants, to this day, especially among the people of the outports.

On the "French Shore" at midnight on Christmas Eve, a live brand from the Yule-log is solemnly taken outdoors and thrown o'er the house, to preserve it from being burned down the coming year. Peculiar observance is given to the crowing of the cock on Christmas night, and it is a common thing in Bonavista Bay to hear people say, when the cock crows in the stillness of Christmas Eve night, "He is scaring away the evil spirits from the Christmas Holy Day." Most people believe too that the cattle kneel at the Manger when the clock strikes twelve.

On Christmas Eve, at Broad Cove (Bonavista Bay) a custom brought from Ireland by the generation of hardy pioneers, long passed away, is still religiously observed, and it is believed to ensure plenty of provisions and good times during the coming year. A loaf of Christmas Bread is cut into four parts by the housewife, and a quarter thrown to each side of the house, indicating plenty from north, south, east and west.

It is also believed that the deer kneel on Christmas night. It is a common thing for those who go in the bottoms of the Bays "on winter works" to stay up all night to watch the caribou kneeling in the snow.

Telling fortunes, by melting lead on Christmas and New Year's nights, is a custom still kept up among the ladies in at least one village in Newfoundland. It is invariably done to obtain some knowledge of what kind of looking fellow the future husband will be. Whether the result will confirm the omen of the cards about the "dark-haired man across the water" is anyone's guess.

The fundamental spirit of the age deals with these old customs and traditions with a ruthless hand. Many of the old customs that our forefathers of Newfoundland observed at Christmas, in the days of the open-fireplace, are looked on by their descendants with ridicule, if not with contempt. Cui bono? After a hard season's work at the fishery, the harmless sports, and relaxation of the Christmas season made new men of them, and a firm religious belief quickened them into close touch with the grand story of the Nativity and made them better Christians. Nonchalant and silent fishermen, who had not a word to say all year round, now blossomed into Grand Knights of St. Patrick, St. Michael and St. George, Hector, Alexander, etc., and gave out their heroic speeches in verse as they went in fantastic mummering custom from one neighbour's house to another. At the village of _____, the last of them passed away to his eternal reward a year ago. Alas! old age and hard work had shrivelled him up to unheroic proportions. But "poor old Tommy Holland" once stood on the floor on Christmas night, a veritable hero, as he recited:

Here Come I Hector, the renowned Hector,
King Priam's only son etc..

May the light of Heaven shine upon them all, this Christmas night.

Newfoundland Christmas Treats

by Alice Lannon

One of the Christmas customs that has come down to us from older times is the baking of sweet bread for Christmas. In fact it is still very much a part of the Christmas celebration in many Newfoundland homes. "Sweet Bread" is a special bread made of flour, molasses and raisins. In the old days it was only made for Christmas. Many Newfoundland writers make mention of this Christmas treat and it is one of the memories of past happier Christmases that haunted Dr. Felix Dowsley as he lay dying of hunger and exposure on Gull Island in 1867.

Sweet bread took longer to rise than ordinary bread and more yeast had to be used. As well the bread had to be baked at a lower oven temperature. It takes about an extra fifteen minutes to bake the "Sweet Bread." An old Newfoundland recipe for "Sweet Bread" is as follows:

Ingredients:
>   3 cups of raisins
>   3 pks or envelopes of fast rising yeast
>   12 cups of all purpose flour
>   2 tablespoons of salt
>   1/2 cup of sugar
>   1 teaspoon of cinnamon
>   2 cups of molasses

1/2 cup of margarine
2 cups of milk

Directions:

Put molasses, milk, butter, sugar and salt in a saucepan. Heat until the butter is melted then cool to lukewarm. In a bowl, put two cups of lukewarm water and two tablespoons of sugar. Stir to dissolve sugar. Then sprinkle the yeast over the top and let stand in a warm place for ten minutes.

Place the flour in a large pan and stir in three cups of either dark or light raisins. Make a hole in the middle of the flour by pushing the flour to the side of the pan. Now pour in the risen yeast mixture and fold in a little flour. Then add the milk and molasses in three additions, mixing the flour well. When it turns to a soft dough, knead well and cover the surface and bottom of the dough with margarine. Cover and let rise until double the original size. This should take about three or four hours. Then knead the dough down again and let rise for another two to three hours. Grease loaf pans and form dough into buns and put in a warm place to rise to about two inches above the rim of the pan. Have oven heated to about 350 F and put pans in the oven leaving a slight space between the pans usually on the middle rack. Bake for forty minutes, turn pans, and bake for another twenty-five minutes. Turn out on a rack to cool and brush with margarine or butter while still warm.

A loaf of this homemade delicacy given to a friend or relative was a very welcomed Christmas gift.

Christmas Pudding

Another special Newfoundland Christmas treat was plum pudding and although Cromwell and his followers classed having plum pudding as being a "papist custom," persons of all religious denominations in Newfoundland and Labrador looked forward to that special Christmas treat. An old recipe for a Christmas pudding that I call Mom's Christmas Pudding goes like this:

Fruit:
   1 cup of seedless raisins
   1 cup of seeded raisins
   1 cup of chopped mixed peel
   1/2 cup of diced citron peel
   1 cup of chopped blanched almonds
   1 cup of chopped dates

Flour & Crumbs (Blend all together, mixing well):
   2 cups of bread crumbs
   1 cup all purpose flour
   1 teaspoon of baking powder
   1 teaspoon of salt
   1 1/2 cups of brown sugar
   1 1/2 cups of chopped suet

Spices:
   1 teaspoon of allspice
   1 teaspoon of cinnamon
   1 teaspoon of nutmeg
   1/2 teaspoon of cloves

Eggs & Flavouring:
   3 eggs
   1 teaspoon of vanilla flavouring

1 teaspoon of almond flavouring
1 teaspoon of lemon flavouring

General Directions:

Combine the fruit mixture and dry ingredients adding the egg mixture a little at a time and stirring well. The dough will be a bit stiff.

Using a square of strong cotton or flour bag 16 to 18 inches square or a pudding bag, place the dough in centre of cloth or bag and tie tightly. Place in a large pot of boiling water with a plate or saucer placed in the bottom to keep the cloth from burning. Cover tightly and boil for three hours adding more boiling water as it evaporates from the pot. At the end of three hours turn out on a plate and let cool. The pudding when cool can be wrapped and kept in the refrigerator for a week before using.

When ready to serve the pudding, it can be heated in a microwave or placed over boiling water until heated. Then serve with a rum sauce.

Rum Sauce for Pudding:

Place two cups of water in a saucepan, add 1/4 cup of butter or margarine, 3/4 cups of white or 1 cup of brown sugar. Bring to a boil and then mix 3 tablespoons of corn starch with 1/4 cup of water to make a thick paste. Stir well and add to saucepan. Cook for four or five minutes stirring to keep the mixture from burning. Remove from heat and cool slightly then add 1/4 cup of rum or sherry wine. Also, if so desired, a teaspoon of vanilla flavouring can be added with the rum. Keep the sauce warm and serve over the pudding.

The Christmas Concert at St. Joseph's, St. Mary's Bay

by Joseph Dobbin

Thinking back over time, I think the earliest memory I have of the Christmas concert is when I was in the "low school." There were two classrooms in our school building which were located on the first floor. The second floor was the Parish Hall, or the "Hall" as everyone called it. It contained a large dance floor, a stage, a small dining room and above the dining room there was a smoking gallery. Children from grades one to grades six were taught in the low school, and those from grades seven to eleven were taught in the high school.

All throughout the month of December, our teachers would be preparing for the big event—the Christmas concert, for St. Stephen's night in the hall upstairs. During our recess breaks and after school was let out at four o'clock, there would be practice. The younger pupils practised first, then the intermediate and then those in the high school. It would be after dark when these practices would be over. These dark evenings (there were no street lights) provided lots of opportunities for courting on the way home.

When the big night finally arrived, the Hall would be filled with long rows of wooden stools. In front of the stage, the teachers placed two of their own chairs which looked like office chairs. They could tip and swivel around. One of these was for the parish priest and the other was for his housekeeper or his close friend, who might be the priest from the nearby parish. All along the walls kerosene lamps cast long shadows onto the audience of parents, grandparents and children. Evergreen boughs in the form of garlands and wreaths decorated the walls and stage.

Even though we didn't know the term "stage hands" then, we did in fact have them, for in order to raise and lower the stage curtains two pairs of strong arms were needed. It was a canvas curtain which was raised and lowered by the use of pulleys and ropes, worked from both ends of the stage, behind the scenes of course.

Perhaps you may remember this curtain; in actual fact it was a painting of Little Harbour, later known as Newbridge. Its artist was a man by the name of Dan Carroll who was well known in the early part of the last century. If you would like to see some of his work today you may visit the halls of Littledale.

In order to gain admittance to this great community event there would be a charge of fifty cents for adults and ten cents for the children who were not "on the stage." Everyone in our community who could attend would be there when the priest came in, then all the assembly stood and remained standing until he took his seat. Then when everyone was seated, the lamps would be turned down and a hush would come over all. The curtain would be raised and the chorus of Jingle Bells would begin accompanied by the teacher on the organ.

One pupil always had an important role to play in each of these concerts. He or she would announce the items. "The first item on the program is the Address of Welcome," and so on.

I remember in part, a recitation which I had one year. Maybe you can recall a line or two. It went like this...

> St. Joseph got mad as a hatter
> And drew himself up full of pride
> If you dare put me out of heaven
> I'll take with me Mary, my bride
> And since she is truly God's mother
> She'll take with her Jesus, her son
> And then there won't be any heaven.
> Said Peter, St. Joseph you've won.

I remember a Nativity scene. It was called a "tableau" and it had all the important characters; Mary, Joseph, the shepherds, the angels and Baby Jesus. Girls' voices were singing in the background, the Christmas songs like *Silent Night* and *Adeste Fideles*.

I remember a little girl in grade one or two whose lines went like this.

> Oh dear! Oh dear!
> I feel so queer
> My heart goes pitty pat
> So, I think I'll make a bow
> And leave you after that.

There would be drills for girls dressed as angels. They would be wearing paper dresses and paper wings and always had to keep in step to a tune. There was also drills for boys. I can recall one called "Ghost March." It was made up of eight boys covered with a white sheet. They were required to march around shivering and speaking their lines in shivery voices. The lines, I believe were:

> Our bones are old
> We're very cold
> We shiver, shiver
> Shake with cold.

Remember the Highland Fling? It was danced to the tune of *Sally Broke the Jam Crock*. Sometimes this was a solo performance, at other times it was a group performance, but it was always danced by girls.

Another recitation coming to mind went like this:

> Little boy kneel at the foot of his bed
> Droops on his little hands, little gold head
> Hush! Hush! Whispers! Who's there?
> Christopher Robin is saying his prayers.

* * *

Because our parish priest was an Irishman, our teachers always included a few Irish songs in these concerts like *How can you buy Killarney?*

I hope by now I've nudged your memory into giving you many more scenes from this enjoyable part of your past.

Newfoundland and Labrador

Christmas Stories

Brave Martin Lane

by Mrs. Anderson

One Christmas night just fifty years ago, a little fishing village not far from St. John's was all astir. Lights twinkled brightly in every window which seemed all the brighter because the night was dark and stormy and there was no white moon to dim their radiance. The day had been fine but frosty. At daybreak men and boys had tackled in the dogs and gone bounding over the snow to get the Christmas logs.

A wide chimneyplace with a settle on either side and long "pot hooks and hangers" descended from a beam with the time honoured kettle and bake pot were all that were necessary for cooking or warmth in those days. Across the "iron dogs" the firs, spruce and birch logs were laid and during the long Newfoundland winters, the settle in the chimney was the cosiest place in the house.

On this particular night, Skipper Joe's cottage was the centre of attention. To it all the people in the harbour, young and old had been bidden, for it was not only that Father Christmas always held high revels and mirth in the place, but Skipper's Joe's only child, Susie was to be married and great was the rejoicing.

Skipper Joe was a big man in the harbour. Not only was he comfortable, owning a goodish bit of land as well as two schooners, but he was a Lay Reader in the church as well. When it came to his lot to read a sermon, there were not many hard words in it that Skipper Joe could not come round.

Susie was not only a good maid, but a clever one and handsome as well. In fact she was a regular village belle. This was Susie's wedding night and great had been the preparations for the event. Aunt Poll, Susie's mother, had been "up to her eyes" as she expressed it for weeks past, kneading and baking and brewing and now it was done. The supper was spread out and what a supper! No words can do justice to the display of good things for with Christmas and a wedding coming off at the same time, Aunt Poll had made almost superhuman efforts on the cooking line and now her face wore a look of pride mingled with a lively anxiety—for was not the pudding still on her mind, there was no knowing how it would turn out until it was in the dish.

Now the guests began to arrive and although Skipper Joe's kitchen was a large one, it was a puzzle to find room for all. Everyone was happy except—strange to say—the bride elect herself who sat lifeless and took very little interest in anything. The bridegroom, a strapping young fisherman, had just come in. He also was an only child and would inherit his father's place and property, and as he was a decent sober lad he was a great favourite with Susie's parents who had done all they could to further the young man's suit.

Everyone knew that Susie's heart had been given to Tom Adams, the schoolmaster's son, but he was wild and three years ago had gone as a sailor on a foreign vessel and had not been heard of since. Some said Susie had no love for Martin Lane although she was to marry him, and as he noticed her downcast looks on the wedding night, he was stricken to the heart for he passionately loved the girl.

"'Tis a stormy night outside," said Skipper Joe, "freezing guns and a heavy gale from the nor'east." Even as he spoke the fine drifting snow struck against the windows of the house and the wind came in heavy gusts shaking the house. The "joy guns" which the men had been firing all day at intervals had ceased and all had gathered for the wedding as the Parson had driven up in his sleigh almost covered with snow.

And now the ceremony was about to begin. Susie and Martin had just taken their places in front of the Parson when suddenly right from the hill on which the cottage stood came two loud reports. At once all was confusion.

"A ship on the rocks," said Skipper Joe with consternation in his voice. In an instant every man was battling through the blinding snow on his way to render every assistance in his power. The women at once proceeded to get hot water and blankets ready. Even the bride gave a helping hand and no one gave a thought to the wedding that had so rudely been interrupted, for there are no kinder hearts in all the world than the hearts of the Newfoundland fisherfolk whose humble doors are always "on the latch" ready to help a stranger in sorrow or distress.

When the men reached the beach, a large vessel was soon seen looming through the darkness and blinding snow. She was drifting helplessly and in a few minutes struck on the rocks.

The sea ran mountainous high, but nothing daunted eight stalwart fishermen who immediately manned a boat and pulled off from the shore. Among them was Martin Lane of whom there was not a more daring seaman in Newfoundland. They rowed for their lives through the raging sea and got as near the vessel as they could just as she parted amidships with a loud report. Dark figures were seen clinging to the masts but the boat could not get any nearer owing to the high seas.

At last Martin Lane volunteered to swim to the wreck with a rope about him and succeeded in saving five souls before the vessel sank beneath the angry waves. Then seeing he could do no more and almost exhausted, brave Martin Lane struck out for the shore and had nearly reached it when he felt himself clutched by the hands of a drowning person.

"Oh! Save me! Save me!" a man's voice entreated, "Do not leave me to die like this so near my home."

"Who are you?" gasped Martin.

"Don't you remember Tom Adams who went away three years ago?" was the almost inarticulate reply, and an even icier chill than that he felt from the bitter waters struck Martin's heart, for like a flash it came to him this was Susie's old love returning and that now he could never have her for his bride. For an instant, but only for an instant he was tempted to shake off his rival and let the dark waves close over Tom's head. But such a brave man could not be guilty of such a cowardly deed, and after a fierce fight in the eye of the storm he succeeded in reaching the shore with his unconscious burden.

It would take too long to tell the confusion caused when Martin and Tom were carried up to Skipper Joe's. How Susie could not conceal her joy at the return of her old love who had come home a reformed and prosperous man. How her joy was turned to grief when a few weeks later Tom was summoned to go on his last voyage from whence there is no return having caught a chill on the night of the wreck from which he never recovered. How before next Christmas Day came round, Susie and Martin were married and how Skipper Joe made his

famous speech and brought down the house when he
referred to the self sacrifice and bravery of Martin Lane.

A Christmas Miracle

by Mike McCarthy

In 1850, the Reverend James Brown, a native of Carbonear was the first native born Newfoundlander to be ordained to the Roman Catholic priesthood in Newfoundland. He was ordained in 1850 by Bishop Mullock and was immediately sent to Northern Newfoundland where his huge parish stretched from Notre Dame Bay round by Quirpon and the Straits of Labrador. For thirty-seven years Reverend Brown faithfully served his scattered congregation. He travelled in open boat, on foot and by dog team. During most of his thirty-seven years of service on the Northeast coast he was the only Roman Catholic priest in the area.

Towards the end of his long years of service to his northern parishioners, Father Brown had an experience that has been preserved as the legend of the "Angel Priest." It was towards the end of his tenure on the Northeast coast when the custom of having Midnight Mass in the Roman Catholic church on Christmas Eve came to Newfoundland. Father Brown decided that he would have a Midnight Mass in his parish church.

In preparation for the event he organized a church choir and encouraged his parishioners to decorate the church with wreaths of pine and fir. The crib was set up and everything was made ready for the first Midnight Mass. The people of the community eagerly looked forward to the novelty of starting off the Christmas Season by attending mass at midnight and a capacity congregation was guaranteed.

Then on Tib's Eve, December 23, Father Brown got a sick call from a community some distance away. Although the glass was falling and the weather was threatening to turn nasty, a sick call could not be put off. He left about noon and it was now clear a storm was brewing. However, used to travelling the coast in all sorts of weather, he paid no attention to the gathering storm and promised that he would be back to the parish church for Midnight Mass on Christmas Eve.

Father Brown made it to the dying person and administered the last sacrament. He was ready to return home when the storm broke in all its fury and he could do nothing but wait it out and hope it cleared in time for him to make it back for Midnight Mass.

His hopes were dashed the next day when the storm increased in violence and he had to admit he would not get back in time for the mass in the parish church.

Back at the Parish centre the people prayed for Father Brown's safety and hoped he wouldn't be foolish enough to try and make it back through the storm. They were also praying that the weather would clear in time for him to get back. But as night closed in, it became evident that the Midnight Mass would have to wait for next year and the people resigned themselves to having to make do with a recitation of the Rosary at midnight.

Despite the poor weather a goodly crowd had gathered at the church and one of the older men who read the Rosary when the priest was absent from the parish, prepared to take his place at the altar rail. However, just before he got up to go up to the Altar, the sacristy door opened and a strange priest, a young man, came out fully vested for mass and ascended the altar steps.

There was great wonderment among the people for they had not known that Father Brown was entertaining a fellow priest. However, they were delighted that despite the storm they would now be able to have their Midnight Mass.

Before beginning the service, the stranger welcomed the people to their first Midnight Mass in the name of their pastor, and said he knew how disappointed Father Brown must be at not being able to be with them on this great occasion because of the storm. He was delighted, he said, to be able to fill in for Father Brown. When he spoke, the people felt a strange sense of peace descending upon them.

Then the choir began to sing and the priest joined in with them. Never had the congregation heard such a voice, and it seemed to them he sang with the voice of an angel.

It was a beautiful mass, and at the end, as the priest turned and blessed the congregation, a great feeling of peace and contentment ran through those who had gathered there to honour the birth of the Christ Child. After the final "Deo gratias" and the prayers after mass, the strange priest and the altar boys went back into the sacristy.

With the natural courtesy of the oldtime, outport Newfoundlander, a number of men when they had finished their prayers of thanksgiving went to the sacristy to thank the stranger and wish him Merry Christmas. He was not in the sacristy, the altar boys said he had disrobed quickly and gone out the back door. The men assumed he must be a bit shy and had gone back to the parish house.

During the night the weather cleared and Father Brown arrived back home just after daylight. He was sorry that he had to disappoint his parishioners and he would now have to say two masses as usual. Coming to the house of the man who helped around the parish, he went in to get him to light the fire in the church stove and ring the bell for early mass.

"You don't need to have an early mass, Father Brown," the man said, "your friend, the young priest, said the Midnight Mass when you didn't get back last night."

"My friend, the young priest," said Father Brown in surprise. "What are you talking about?"

The old man told him about the strange priest coming out and saying mass, and about the beautiful singing. "All hands agreed, Father," said the man. "He had the voice of an angel."

The old priest thought for a moment. The nearest Roman Catholic priest was more than one hundred miles away, and it was impossible for him to have journeyed so far at that time of the year. Then, suddenly he knew, God in his mercy had sent an Angel priest to help him out and reward the faith of his people.

He didn't tell the parish worker what he was thinking, only wished him a holy and happy Christmas and asked him to heat the church and ring the bell for the late mass.

Before going to the parish house he entered the church and kneeling before the altar thanked God for sending an angel to help an old man in a time of need.

Father Brown never told his people of the great miracle they had been a part of except to say that God had blessed them in ways that were beyond the comprehension of mortal man. Many years later in his last parish in Harbour Main he did tell the story to his curate, and it is from that source that the legend of the Christmas Miracle on the Northeast Coast has come down to us.

A Strange Christmas Box

by J. W. Kinsella

Jimmy Hemmings was a Newfoundlander—a Newfoundlander in every sense of the word—and his father's great-grandfather was a Newfoundlander too. Of course this wasn't true, but Hemmings said it was and boasted of it, for which we must admire the man's memory the more. The last day of Jimmy's journey on this earthly sphere was the 14th of February, 1800. We come to this conclusion because on a rough slab over his grave is the following inscription. "To the Memory of Jimmy only son of and child of Jacob Hemmings who died on Valentine's Day, 1800."

To be sure it reads a little ambiguous, and would lead one to think 'twas Jacob died on Valentine's Day; but strict inquiry and a thorough search of the church registry have cleared all doubts on this point, and we can now with safety assure the whole world that it was Jimmy, the hero of this sketch, that shuffled off this mortal coil on St. Valentine's Day.

But as it is Mr. Hemmings in the flesh we have to do with, we'll drop all talk of his demise and inscription, and get on, without any further interruptions to our tale.

Besides boasting of being a Terra Novian, Jimmy had other things to be proud of: he was monarch of all the surrounding settlements, in as much as he was schoolmaster and postmaster; priest and parson; judge, lawyer and jury; and the terror, righteously, of all adjacent posts, and his word from Cape Ray to Cape Bauld was unquestioned.

But, with all these posts of trust and honour, alas! for poor Hemmings, he possessed his weak point too — he fell in love, and with that fell all his greatness, all his noble avocations and was ultimately robbed of his popularity and independence.

But, had Mr. Hemmings' passion been reciprocated, perhaps in his own estimation, 'twould be an acceptable equivalent for all his losses. But not so. Jimmy's inamorata, Alice Palfrey, loved Jimmy's own cousin, and bed fellow, and partner in fish matters (Jacob Jeffers) too well, and while poor Hemmings was trying to make up his mind to declare himself, Jeffers proposed, and was accepted, and married all in one breath.

This severed all business connections between the two rivals. The firm of Hemmings and Jeffers became a thing of the past, though each followed his usual avocation, as the neighbours termed it "on his own bottom."

Alice Palfrey and Jacob Jeffers hadn't been married a month, when a big uproar was made in the little village of _____. All the boats had returned from the fishing grounds, and Jacob Jeffers' skiff had been seen bottom up, and fears were entertained for the worst. And when all hopes had been given up, and a too long time had elapsed ever to expect poor Jeffers in their midst again, people began to whisper to each other, and point out the advantage such a death was to Hemmings.

But what could they do? Hemmings was the law, he was the bench, the bar and the jury; and in fact the whole government machinery. Although one of the fisherfolk heard loud words between the rivals that fatal day on the fishing grounds, no one would attempt to openly accuse Jimmy of doing away with Jeffers. But the thing looked suspicious, and so full of advantage to Hemmings, that they no longer recognized him as law-maker, and from that day wrestled from him the bench, the bar, and the pulpit.

And silently did poor old Jimmy accept the stigma, but not without feeling within himself sufficiently to say: "These people believe me to be the murderer of Jeffers, and I have no way to prove to them how inno-cent I am."

One year has passed, and now we see Hemmings again making overtures to the widow Jeffers, who is still comely and winning and the mother of a fine young Jeffers, three months old.

Here is a part of the wooing:

"Will you Alice?"

"No, Jimmy, I'll never give Jacob's boy a stepfather; and besides, I needn't tell you Hemmings, that people believe you and Jacob were angry that day, and, well, they never trusted you since."

"Did you believe as they did Alice?"

"No Jimmy."

"And won't you give me any hope?"

"No, Jimmy. It might be different if I hadn't Jacob's boy."

And thus, day after day, month in and month out, Hemmings pleaded and Mrs. Jeffers refused, until six months more had passed and Alice's child was nine months old.

One morning, Hemmings had just moored his boat and was going to his home with a few fresh fish hung over his shoulder, when he saw smoke issuing from the window of Mrs. Jeffers' dwelling. It was very early, too early for the usual morning fire, and Jimmy hurried with all his might. Rushing in, he saw the place was in a mass of flames, with no one apparently in the house, but the child sleeping innocently in his cot.

Like lightening, Alice's words came to his mind, "*It might be different if I hadn't Jacob's boy.*" He made no out-cry, but grasped the child, and with no one living within hearing distance from the burning house, Hemmings and his charge escaped unseen. One hour after, Jimmy Hemmings and Jacob Jeffers' child were sleeping soundly at Hemmings' home regardless of the cries and moans of poor Mrs. Jeffers, who on returning, after fill-ing her pail with water from the river, saw her home in ashes, and as she believed her child was in ashes too.

But as we cannot comfort Mrs. Jeffers in her great sorrow by telling her of her boy's safety, we must only pass over another two or three months, and find Mr. Jimmy Hemmings once more making love to the still fair widow in another aspect. Here is a dialogue of some of the wooing.

"Will you now, Alice?"

"No, Jimmy; I'm alone in the world now; my great sorrow has killed all affection in me. Now, if little Jacob had been spared me, I might be induced to accept a bread-earner and protector for him; but now; oh, no, Mr. Hemmings; never now."

"But Alice —"

"No use, Jimmy; my heart is buried with the two Jacobs."

That night Jimmy was in his house a sorrowful man. "What have I done," said he. "Made life not worth living for the one woman I love. Brought sorrow and sadness upon her; robbed her of her child, the one living thing by which, from her own lips, I might have won her. But I did it with good intentions, and when I restore the child to its mother, that child will plead for me, and with its great love for me, I swear before heaven tonight that I will wed its mother."

With this resolution, Jimmy retired to his accustomed apartment at the side of his adopted boy; and the talk of the village for the next two years was, "what has come over Hemmings; he's not been seen on the path as usual, and hasn't even visited the fishing grounds as was his wont; what has changed him?" But Jimmy was giving his life to win the big love of Alice Jeffers' child, because through the child he thought he could best accomplish his end. And, indeed, he lavished all the kindness and all the endearments of father and mother to the little one; not leaving it morning or night, doing for it, and teaching it, so that when the young one was five years old, he would not allow his father — as he termed him — a moment out of his sight. Thus, Jimmy admirably won in winning all the child's love and admiration to a degree that in part satisfied him for the slight he felt by the refusals received from Jacob's mother.

But the time was ripening now for Hemmings' last throw; he felt sure to win the mother through the child. The child loved him and would not leave him for all the world. But how was he going to approach his old love with the new? A thought struck him! Yes, the very thing! Next week would bring Christmas. Christmas, when peace and happiness and good-will, and rejoicing, and new blessings are given to all.

"On Christmas Eve, I'll present Alice with a Christmas box — that gift shall be her son — and — and — and, yes, and mine. The son will plead for the father, because he thinks I am his father, and he loves me. Alice — his mother — in her joy and happiness will listen to the voice of our son — and, by the holy sailor, I'll win."

'Tis six o'clock on Christmas Eve. Alice Jeffers sits alone over her Christmas fire. She is lonesome and sad; her life is desolate. Other homes are bright and happy; gladness is seen and heard on every hearth. What has the future for her? Nothing! What does tomorrow bring her; the great and welcomed Christmas morning, when the whole world will shout in gladness—and here she breaks down under her sorrow and bursts into tears.

At that moment the door opens and Hemmings is standing by her side. "What is it Alice? This is not the season for crying. The whole village is aglow and happy, and celebrating Christmas Eve. Come, be cheerful; I have a Christmas box for you. One that you will like, and one that will make you happy!"

"'Tis kind of you Jimmy to think of me in that way. I do not deserve it; but nothing can ever again make me happy."

"Come, come, Alice. Your Christmas box is at my house; come and accept it."

"I cannot, Jimmy, please go and leave me tonight; for this night of all others when everyone is rejoicing, I am more sad."

"Come, Alice, come! No such Christmas box has ever been given to anyone before. Come, 'twill make you happy."

His earnestness and change of manner struck her. She immediately rose, and both, amidst the shouts of children sliding and enjoying the frosty air of this Christmas Eve, proceeded towards the dwelling of Hemmings where indeed the woman was to receive such a Christmas box that the joy of it ever lived in her memory through her long and happy life.

When they arrived at the door Hemmings pointed and said, "Go in, Alice, and in that room your present awaits you." At any other time she would hesitate, and would not enter Hemmings' house alone. But something urged, to an unknown voice whispered, trust him, and opening the door she entered the room. But Hemmings turned away from the dwelling, fearing the meeting of the child and mother, or fearing, perhaps, the part he took in the separation.

An hour afterwards he stealthily approached the door, and on entering, beheld the mother sobbing over the child, and he with his arms clasped around her neck, both enjoying the most bright, and heavenly and cheering Christmas that ever fell to the lot of mortals here below.

And when the holidays had passed, and those three had spent the happy festival together in unity and gladness, and when the mother saw the devotion and reverence her boy had for the man who saved his life; and when she heard with childish prattle, how Hemmings had never tired of telling the child of its mother, and taught him to love her as he himself loved, the visits of Jimmy were more favourably looked upon. And when, once more Hemmings with the child clinging to his shoulders, asked for her hand, she smiling reached it to him over the little one, and said:

"You have given a great blessing to my days. You have restored my son from the grave, and for that gift, here is my hand, my love, and my life, accept them in return for yours to me as my Christmas box."

A Child's Christmas Prayer

by J. W. Foley

Dear Lord be good to Santa Claus,
He's been so good to me;
I've never told him so because
He is so hard to see.
He must love little children so
To come through snow and storm;
Please care for him when cold winds blow
And keep him nice and warm.

Dear Lord, be good to him and good
To Mary Christmas too
I'd like to tell them, if I could,
The things I'm telling you.
They've both been very good to me,
And everywhere they go
They make us glad; no wonder we
All learn to love them so.

Please have him button up his coat
So it will keep him warm;
And wear a scarf around his throat
If it should start to storm.
And when the night is dark, please lend
Him light if stars are dim,
Or maybe sometimes you could send
An angel down with him.

Please keep his heart so good and kind
That he will always smile;
And tell him we will find
And thank him after a while.
Please keep him safe from harm and keep
Quite near and guard him when
He's tired and lays him down to sleep.
Dear Lord, please do!

                     Amen.

Nellie's Christmas

Anonymous

The autumn of 1873 had been a remarkable fine one, but now winter had commenced his rigorous reign in good earnest, and though a day or two before everyone was saying it would be a green Christmas, a shift of wind to the north and a continuous fall of snow for some hours had effected a complete change in the aspects of nature. The black beetling cliffs, projecting crags and huge boulders, which formed the most prominent feature of the scenery around Shelter Cove, a little fishing settlement on the northeast coast of Newfoundland, were now covered with a mantle, of purest white, which softened their rugged and almost forbidding appearance. As the short day drew to its close, and the storm cleared, and the setting sun cast its slanting rays on cliff and crag, and housetops, glinting and glistening in their snowy cover, it seemed beautiful as a scene from fairyland.

On this winter evening, the village was a scene of busy activity. The stalwart fishermen engaged in cutting up wood for fuel, for tomorrow would be Christmas Day and a good stock must be laid in; but especially must the "Christmas brand" or "Yule Log" be prepared and lodged in its position across the dog irons.

The sound of the axes rang out cheerily on the frosty air, while ever and anon, blending with it, came the report of firearms with which the younger members of the community welcomed the joyous Advent time. The savory whiffs, which came forth as the cottage doors were opened, plainly indicated that the good wife was actively engaged within making preparations for the festive season.

One house alone seems exempt from this cheerful hum of preparation. Larger and more pretentious than its neighbours, it indicated that its builders must have been men of some means, while an appearance of neglect and decay as plainly indicated that its present occupants were not basking in the sunshine of prosperity. On entering it we find ourselves in a capacious kitchen, one side of which is entirely occupied by a large old fashioned fireplace, in which a wood fire is burning; its cheery but fitful light, one moment revealing, and the next leaving in shadows, the dark wainscotted walls, the scanty furniture, and the sanded floor neatly swept in zig-zag lines, according to the custom of the times.

On a bench, or settle, by a fire, we observe a man in a half sitting, half recumbent position. The firelight flashes across his features one on whom age, care and sickness have traced their indelible footprints.

There is but one other occupant of the room, a fair-haired, blue-eyed girl of twelve years, meanly and thinly clad, but possessing a face of wondrous beauty, and a sylph-like figure of surpassing gracefulness. She has just laid their evening meal on a small table in such a position that the aged invalid might partake of the repast without moving from his seat, and the gentleness of her movements, and thoughtful kindness of her manner, show that her attendance on him is a labour of love.

There is little to tempt the appetite of a sick person, the food being of the coarsest description, and after sipping a cup of tea, the old man lies back on his couch and watches his little attendant as she deftly and quickly clears away the tea-things. Having done so, and taking some sewing, she seats herself on a low stool, close by him, saying, "Grandfather, are you warm enough or shall I get something to lay over you?"

"I am quite warm, my dear, with that fire." As he speaks he lays his feeble hand on her head saying, "Nellie, my darling, my only earthly comfort, this is a sad and lonely Christmas Eve! Last year your dear grandmother was with us, but now she lies yonder in the graveyard, and only you and I are left, Nellie. Tonight my thoughts go back to the time when I led her forth from this very house, a fair young bride. The world went well with me then, Nellie! I was master and owner of as fine a brig as sailed out of St. John's, and fortune smiled on me for many years. Your father and your uncle John grew up strong and brave, and true, such sons as any father might be proud of. But as time passed the seal fishery began to fail, and the steamers soon drove our noble fleet of sailing vessels out of the business.

"I lost a considerable amount, but was still in comfortable circumstances. I owned a snug home in St. John's, and the old brig (rebuilt and as good as new) was engaged in the foreign trade, under your father's command, your uncle being with him as mate.

"Ten years ago last October, your father sailed for the Mediterranean, taking your mother with him, but leaving you, a tiny tot of two in our care.

"That was a stormy season on the Atlantic, and many a good ship went down, your father's among them, and the mail by which we expected news of their safe arrival brought tidings of wreckage in mid-ocean, which too plainly indicated that they had been engulfed in the merciless sea. Then, while we were in the midst of this sorrow, the firm of Transfer & Co. failed, and I was left penniless. In the Spring, I sold my place in St. John's and with the proceeds commenced a small business in this place, as this house and premises had been inherited by your grandmother.

"Failing fisheries however soon swallowed it all up, but I still straggled on, battling with adversity until last spring, when your dear grandmother died, then it seemed as my life was gone, strength and energy failed me; and ever since I have been growing weaker day by day, until at last, Nellie darling, I am face to face with sickness and gaunt starvation. Everything saleable has gone for food. I have striven to the last, and now the most bitter trial of all has come. Tomorrow, Nellie, I must apply for the pauper's dole. Oh, it is hard! Hard! Hard! But God's will be done." The old man arose with difficulty, and tottering across the kitchen to his room, threw himself upon his bed to indulge his grief alone.

Nellie sometimes sat gazing into the fire with tear-dimmed eyes. "Poor dear grandpa," she murmured. "O, how I wish I could do something to help him." Then rising, as if a sudden thought had crossed her mind, she said, "There's that ring that mother left behind her, I'll take that to Mr. Waden, the trader, and get something nice for grandpa's Christmas dinner, but I must not let him know." She then crept to the door of his room, and found that he had fallen asleep, covering him up carefully, and hurriedly dressing herself as warmly as her scanty wardrobe would permit, she started on her errand.

There was no moon, but the stars were twinkling brightly in the clear sky, except to the westward where a black cloud bank was rising. A sharp keen west wind was blowing, but calling "Nep" a large black dog came bounding towards her, and she pushed bravely on her way. The distance was not far, but the road was black and dangerous, as it wound the seaward slope of the hills, and about midway a bridge spanned a small brook which came rushing down the hill-side and sprang with a clear leap of fifty feet into the sea. Just as she reached this point, the squall (which had been rising swiftly but unnoticed by her) burst upon her in all its fury. Bewildered, breathless, she endeavoured to press on, but in vain. She turned to retreat, but in a moment was hurled prostrate on the icy bridge, slipped under the railing, and with a cry of terror fell into the gulch below. Providentially, a jutting crag about ten feet below, on which the snow had gathered, intercepted her fall, and she lay unhurt but terrified at the thought that the slightest motion would precipitate her into the yawning gulf beneath.

The noble dog soon made his way to her side and lying down by her endeavoured to protect her from the fury of the elements. Nellie nestled close to her shaggy friend, but the fatal sleep which precedes death from cold began to steal on her.

Suddenly Nep sprang up at the sound of footsteps, and bounding up the cliff confronted a strong looking-man of middle age. The faithful animal soon made him understand that help was needed, and on looking over the bridge he saw the perilous position of the child. Cautiously following in the tracks of the dog, he soon reached the spot where she lay, and lifting her in his strong arms succeeded in bring her to the road. Still following the dog he soon reached Nellie's home, and bringing her into the firelight found that she had fainted. Seeing no one, he laid her on the bench and called aloud for help; then he began briskly rubbing her hands to restore circulation. As he did so the ring fell from them on the hearth, picking it up he glanced at it, and as he did so a strange change came over him, his face becoming white as the child's at his side. He held it nearer the light, examined it closely, and clasping his hands with emotion, exclaimed, "O God, I thank thee!" then gazing a moment with intense interest on the still unconscious child, clasped her in his arms, covering the sweet, pale face with kisses.

Nellie's grandfather had been awakened by the sound of footsteps, and as the call for help fell on his ear, he started up as one in a dream, then with a vigour, that an hour ago he had seemed incapable of, went forward to the kitchen. One moment he gazed on the form by the fire, then crying, "Ned! Ned! My lost boy, has the sea given up its dead?" He tottered forward with outstretched arms and would have fallen had not the stranger quickly caught him in his arms, crying: "Thank God, father, I have found you at last."

Reader my tale is told. I would like to tell you of Nellie's father—of his battle for life with the angry seas, clinging for hours to a broken spar, of his rescue by a ship bound to Australia, of his struggles and trials, and ultimate prosperity in that far off land, of letters failing to reach their destination. All this and more I would like to tell but for the editor's inexorable edict "Not over 2,000 words!"

If you desire to know more of Nellie, seek her among the fairest and most honoured of the fairest daughters of Terra Nova, and she will tell you that many a happy Christmas has she enjoyed since then—one especially, when orange blossoms were mingled with holly and mistletoe. But above all others, she cherishes the memory of that which is called by all who know her, "Nellie's Christmas."

George Skinner's Christmas

by P. K. D.

The fishery at King's Cove in the summer of 18— was very bad, and at the close of the season the catch was only half the average. The price had fallen from twenty-five to twelve shillings a quintal.

The winter set in with unusual severity, and in November the thermometer went down to fifteen degrees below zero. Most of the fishermen in desperation made up their minds early in September not to bring their fish to their merchants at St. John's, but to sell it to traders and buy enough grub for the winter. "Self preservation," said they, "is the first law of nature." They were in debt to the merchant and feared that should they turn in their fish they would get no provisions to bring home, as it would take all they had caught and more, to pay their summer account. Nearly all the planters and fishermen acted accordingly. Even the supply bought from the trader was in most cases, insufficient to tide them over the winter.

"I'm afraid it's going to be a poor Christmas with us this year, boys," said Skipper Joe Holloway, "not even a drop in the jar."

Slade Elson & Company, merchants at St. John's, waited in vain for King's Cove dealers to come along or send along their fish and oil. Finally they heard that the fish and oil had been sold to itinerant merchant traders and there was nothing for them.

The Branch house at Trinity had sent out the news. The firm at St. John's decided to have satisfaction and made up their minds to attach the property of the delinquent dealers at King's Cove.

Three weeks before Christmas, they called their confidential man, George Skinner, into the office and asked him if he was willing to make the journey to King's Cove overland, and privately get an inventory of all property, such as boats, stores, and fishing gear of the dealers, and report. Mr. Skinner replied that he was ready to go, and a clerk was at once sent to make out duplicate copies of certain accounts in the ledger. He was requested by Mr. Slade to send in by first mail, a faithful account of the dealers' condition.

On the 4th of December he left St. John's in the mail coach, equipped as if he was going to the North Pole. At that time a journey to Bonavista Bay in winter was so rarely made that the man who accomplished it was ever after regarded as a hero. Mr. Skinner knew that if he was successful in getting to King's Cove and back, he could lie on his laurels the rest of his life and would be then justified in aspiring to the hand of the niece of the junior partner of the firm.

Harbour Grace was reached, via the head of the bay, and Brigus without any incident of note. Resting four days at that then thriving town beneath the friendly shelter of the "Rutherford Ram," he took a sleigh and dog passage overland to New Perlican via Heart's Content barrens.

Mr. Skinner was lucky to escape a terrible blizzard that came on the night he reached New Perlican. He had great difficulty in finding a place to put up at, but finally the hospitable shipbuilder Skipper George Pittman took him in. There was one boarding house in the village, but it was already taken up with a crew of Punton & Munn's dealers belonging to King's Cove who had been paid off and left their schooner at Harbour Grace. They had fished at Sandy Islands, Labrador, and had done well. All were now waiting on the chance that Peter Coleman's pacquet would come up from Trinity once more before the bay froze over, and take them across. Luckily, a few days before Christmas "the hard spurt" appeared to be over and the weather turned mild. On the 21st the long looked for pacquet hove in sight and on the 22nd the weather had become quite mild and a fair wind to Trinity sprung up from the south.

It was a beautiful evening as the schooner dropped out of the harbour wing and wing. The moon rose and spread a broad golden sheen over the bay. The spirits of the crew of the *Ellen Munn* who were on board, rose high at the thoughts of getting home for Christmas. Even the erstwhile silent passenger, Mr. George Skinner, was moved by the influence of the hour and struck up the popular song, *Jamie on the Stormy Seas*, as he paced the after deck. When he had finished, Joe Doyle of the *Ellen Munn* remarked to Bill McGrath. "Bill, that's a complete song and I'd like to have it. I don't believe there's a new song in our place for the winter."

Bill shook his head. It was as if he fully appreciated the terrible misfortune. "I wonder," he said, after reflecting a bit, "would he write it off for us if we ask him?"

George Doherty, the second mate of the pacquet who was standing by the foremast and heard the conversation, said, "That fellow got a whole bundle of songs in his port-mantial. He showed 'em to me before supper down in the cabin. He said he's a play actor and he's going to get up some concerts in Trinity."

The Skipper then yelled out to let the foresail come over and nothing further was said, but Joe Doyle made up his mind then and there he would not go home without a few new songs for Christmas. He took Bill McGrath into his confidence and made him volunteer to take a trick at the wheel coming on daylight.

When nearing Skerwink, Bill saw Joe coming up out of the cabin with a bundle of papers stuffed under his jumper.

"Keep her along to that Bill," he said, as he went forward to the forecastle. Now Joe was a poor hand at reading, but Bill was a scholar, so when his watch at the wheel was over, he was invited forward to have a look at the songs. The first one he examined was headed "William Sampson & Sons Dr. to Slade Eleson & Co." He was about to utter a cry of surprise when he caught himself and said, "Be the maccle cat, Joe, they're beautiful here to be sure." *Down by the Slaney Side, Hard Hearted Barber Ellen, Brennan on the Moor.*

"Won't we have it up to Uncle Davy Ryan's this Christmas." Joe laughed at it and stowed the papers away in the bosom of his jumper.

Arriving at Trinity the crew of the *Ellen Munn* lost no time in getting on the road to King's Cove, eighteen miles across the country. The echo of the Christmas Eve preparations reached their ears as they descended the valley leading into the village. The sound of the saws and the hatchets cutting Christmas back-junks re-echoed on the frosty air, and a scattered man from the Coves was met going home with his jar.

"It don't look so bad after all after a poor fishery," said Joe Doyle. Just then the booming of a hundred sealing guns was heard reverberating on the still evening air. "There goes auld Slade's powder," said Joe. His companion made no response as he was doing some hard thinking on his own account. He had heard before he left Trinity that Mr. Santoni, the comic reciter (Skinner) had decided to give his first performance in King's Cove and would come over that evening.

"Well done b'ys, keep it up," said Joe as he met up with a crowd of young fishermen at the corner of the beach who were loading their guns for a final volley to fire in the new Christmas.

"What's the news? Will the mummers be out this year?"

"No, Joe," said Jim Carroll with a rueful sigh, "they say we'll have to put it off till New Year's night and perhaps not have it then." "Why is that?" queried Joe.

"Oh you see Ned Martin, who was to take the part of King Priam of Troy, is sick and won't be able to take part. Martin Herrigan who was to take the part of Julius Caesar went up the bay to lay up the *Triton* for the winter, but got jammed at Little Denier for a week, but he got free and will be down this evening. Alexander, Hercules and George Washington, they're all right, but I can't get ahead without King Priam.

Bill McGrath now saw his opportunity. "The man you want is on his way from Trinity and ought to make a good King Priam. He's a jim dandy at play acting and could learn the part in ten minutes. He's a nice fellow, boys and will do anything, all you got to do is to ask him."

Napoleon and Alexander went off to meet with Mr. Santoni. Bill McGrath had gone round to the principal boarding house in which were all the dealers of Slade Elson & Co. He found a letter of instructions among the songs and he used it to carry out his plan.

Santoni, alias Mr. George Skinner, duly arrived but could not get anyone to take him in; they had no room. Only for the kindness of the leaders of the mummers, Alexander and Napoleon, he would have had to walk the streets all night. They would entertain him on one condition; that he would take the part of King Priam and go with them in the mummers.

George made a virtue of extreme necessity and two hours afterwards was transformed into the King of Troy.

Tradition says to this day he was the best they ever had. He entered into the full spirit of the role and in verity became a changed man, but not to do him justice without asking himself was he becoming crazy. When he found he had lost his accounts and papers, he was ready to quit. However the letter written to Slade Eleson & Co. by the next mail contained extracts such as these: "I won't leave this place until next spring and perhaps not then. You fixed me for certain when you sent me here. I'm not George Skinner now, but I'm King Priam and tell the boys in the office not to forget it. Your talking about your dealers down here, let me tell you that George Holloway is King Alexander, William Sampson is Napoleon, Tim Sullivan is George Washington and what do you think, but little Martin Herrigan who always wanted tilly on every tub of salt is none other than Julius Caesar himself. All is lost. I don't know what will become of me, but let me tell you one thing I have never spent so grand a Christmas in all my life."

The Boy Who Almost Got Nothing for Christmas

by Alice Lannon

Timmy was a little boy of seven years. He lived with his parents and he had one sister older than him and a younger brother and sister.

Timmy wasn't really bad. He was mischievous and liked teasing his siblings. Hiding the girls' dolls and occasionally pulling lightly on the girls' hair, or taking his little brother's toys or books. Occasionally he also took some of their treats when his were all gone before theirs.

His poor mother was driven nearly to distraction with complaints from the other children about what Timmy was doing to them. Then, one night in early December when Timmy had been worse than usual, the mother called all the children together.

"Do you know that Santa's Brownies and Elves are watching to see who is being good or bad? They sit on the window ledges and peep through the windows. They have a pencil and pad and if someone is acting naughty a big black mark goes next to the name of the naughty child. If a child is good a gold star goes next to their name.

"Just before Christmas Eve this list is brought to Santa and if there are more black marks than gold stars that child will not get all he or she asked for Christmas and could even end up with an empty stocking Christmas Morning."

After his mother's warning Timmy tried to be good, but it wasn't easy to break bad habits and he continued to tease and torment his brother and sisters. Even on Christmas Eve his mother had to tell him to be good more than once.

That night the stockings were hung up and the children bathed and got ready for bed. Their mother asked them not to come down stairs too early for they might interrupt Santa filling the stockings and if this happened, Santa would have to leave even if some stockings were still empty.

Timmy awoke early Christmas morning even before it was light. He slipped out of bed and crept down the stairs with the intention of snitching a few grapes from the others' stockings as the grapes were usually at the top.

When he went in the living room he saw the stockings hanging by the fireplace. There was his big sister's stocking all bumps and humps with things sticking out of the top and gifts too big for the stocking were under it on the floor. He saw the stockings of his younger brother and sister and they were filled to overflowing with gifts on the floor. Then, he saw his own stocking, flat as a pancake, not even a candy out in the toe. Well! he couldn't believe his eyes, he had to feel the stocking to make sure it was really empty. He was in shock and tears began to flow down his cheeks and he wished he had listened to his mother's warning.

Still in shock he sat on the bottom step of the stairs with his head in his hands and wept silently. Then, a soft voice said in his ear, "What's the matter? No one should be sad on Christmas Day."

Timmy uncovered his eyes and looked up into the face of a little Christmas fairy. He told her what had happened and how sorry he was for having been a bad boy. The fairy looked at him and said, "Because you are sorry for your bad actions, and if you promise me that you will start being good from now on to your brother and sisters, and obey your Mom and Dad, I'll go after Santa and see if he has anything left in his bag. You may not get what you asked for, but I'll see what I can do. Now, you go back to bed and wait until your brother and sisters get up."

Poor Timmy crept back up stairs and got into bed and quietly sobbed himself to sleep. He was awakened by his little brother calling him to get up and go down to see what Santa had left. His heart was heavy and he was the last to enter the living room. He was almost afraid to look at his stocking. Then, his sister asked, "What did you get Timmy?"

Then he looked and his stocking was full of gifts just like the others. He hurried to look and there was a puzzle, a ball, a game and some books. It wasn't what he had asked for, but he was so glad to get a full stocking. He didn't care what the gifts were.

From that day on his mother noticed a big change in Timmy. He played with his younger brother and his sisters and didn't tease them anymore. He was much more helpful to his mother even offering to pick up the wrapping paper and helping his little brother get dressed for dinner. He also helped his sisters set the dinner table.

That night, his mother praised him. "Timmy you were such a good boy today, I hope you keep it up." Timmy told her he was turning over a new leaf which made his mom very happy.

Timmy kept his promise to the Christmas fairy and the next Christmas he got all he asked Santa for and more. He actually set a good example for his brother and sisters which made everyone in the family very happy.

Christmas Memories of

Newfoundland and Labrador

Christmas at St. Lewis Bay Trading Post, Labrador (1850s)

by Lambert De Boilieu

At Christmas the men have eight days holiday, when all sorts of rough sports are carried on. I say rough, because of the forfeits, beginning with rum, invariably end in what is termed a "cobbing;" which means a dozen strokes across the soles of the feet with a wooden slice. Should any one of the crew absent himself from home on Christmas Eve, a deputation from the remainder will be sent in search of him, and when found—even should he be enjoying himself at the big house or the cooperage—he is unceremoniously told to return to his home, and immediately he leaves the house the deputation commences chastising him across the shoulders with old shoes, until he reaches the dwelling where the crew are located, where he undergoes a trial for his desertion, and as a matter of course, as it is Christmastime, he is fined one or two gallons of rum. Frequently more than one absented themselves, just for the sake of being fined, and to give more drink to the rest. The house the crew lives in is fitted up in the dormitory exactly like a ship, with fifteen to twenty berths closed at the ends and open in the centre.

A favourite Christmas game amongst the men, enacted nearly every night during the holidays, is—or was—one called "Sir Samuel and his man Samuel," in which you are to obey the orders of the first, but not of the second. Consequently, when Sir Samuel gives an order, his man contradicts it, and whoever obeys the latter becomes the object of "after-consideration," which means that he is physically punished, fined or given some laborious task to perform. I have seen the last carried out to the delight of many, on a lazy drone who was always skulking his work. His forfeit, however nearly cost him his life. He was condemned to supply the room with six turns of wood; implying he should go to the stack of wood six times, which was at the foot of the hill about three hundred yards off, and he knew he would have no peace until his task was completed, away he went on his errand. I cannot well describe the night. The snow was dense in the air and thick on the ground, and the cold was bitter and biting. Moreover, on the day before, an extraordinarily large quantity of snow had fallen, and from the extreme coldness of the atmosphere, it had become as fine as the sand on the coast of Africa, and as the wind came on to blow in the evening, it commenced drifting or flying in perfect whirlwinds. Only those who have witnessed a snow-drift in this form can conceive what it is like. It blinds, it bewilders one, continually scudding round you, and making you white as the ground. Now this poor lazy fellow had made one trip with great difficulty, and proceeded on the next journey. Not returning as soon as it was thought he ought to, a lantern was procured, and on issuing from the house and seeing the state of the night, the practical jokers began to get alarmed. Although as I have said the pile of wood was only about three hundred yards distant, none dared go to it without a guide. This guide is not a living but an artificial one. A ball of twine is procured and one end made fast to the door-post and the other held in the hand of the "adventurer." One of the crew with this guide went to the wood pile, but when it was reached the missing man was not there. The whole of them went with the same result. To attempt to trace him was out of the question; to "halloo" was useless, as the roar of the wind was awful. Fortunately the man himself caught a glimpse of the lantern and made for it and returned home.

It is at Christmas that the old hands make their almanacs. I can best explain how this is done by giving the information as I received it. "Why you see," said an old fellow, "I got this here board and makes my almanac upon that. I divides the first day after Christmas into four parts, and takes notes of the quarter the wind blows from, and makes my observations on the same, and calls that January—each quarter o' the day represents a week; and I do the same up to the sixth of January, being twelve days after Christmas. I considers them there twelve days represents the twelve months of the year, and as I have made these almanacs for forty years and have always found them true. You can laugh as much as you like."

I must confess the owner of this almanac was always an authority as how the summer would turn out, the time the coast would be clear of ice, what sort of fall it would be, etc. I visited the old man's quarters and there I found, transferred from his board to the side of his room, sundry queer hieroglyphics which he said he understood well himself, and which I daresay he did. Coupled with the wolf's head, this primitive way of rivalling Murphy somewhat impressed me; at all events, I have seen enough to know that only fools laugh at the simple lore of old folk.

How I spent Christmas on the French Shore (1881)

by Reverend T. E. Lynch C. C.

"I must reach Conche before Christmas Day." Such were my thoughts as I sprang from bed on the morning of 23rd December 1884. I was then at a small settlement called Cat's Cove, four miles south of Canada Head. After consulting with my fellow-travellers as to the practicability of such an attempt, we summoned our host and informed him of our resolution. Immediately all is excitement and bustle. The clatter of dishes and the noise of women hurrying to and fro, are mingled with the yelping of dogs, the cracking of whips, and the cries of our guides, as they prepare their teams for the road.

After a hurried breakfast we encased our feet in Indian moccasins, fastened on our snow shoes, pulled on our caps tightly drawn down over our ears and biding adieu to our kind host, we step forth into the morning air; and oh what a morning and what a scene met our gaze!

The sun in all his glorious splendour had just risen above the horizon; not a shadow of a cloud stained the face of the azure sky; not a breath of air kissed our cheeks; yet a delicious sense of invigorating freshness sent the blood coursing rapidly through our veins. A fleecy vapour was rising lazily from the bosom of the slumbering ocean as if loath to quit her motherly embrace. Her bosom was dotted with ice-bergs of the most fantastic shapes. Around the semicircle basin that formed the harbour perched in out-of-the-way places, and on dizzy heights, stood the few log-houses that constitute the settlement. Behind these the barren rock, or dangerous swamp, now buried deeply beneath its snowy covering; and away in the distant back-ground, the dark outlines of the fir forest. Such were the first sights that met my view on this memorable morning. With hearts bounding with delight we are off, admist the huzzas of the children and the salvos of musketry from the young men.

Like lightening our twelve Indian dogs draw us past crag and swamp and lake, and stop at the entrance to the dark forest just spoken of. Then the dogs are unharnessed, our snowshoes carefully examined, our belts tightened around the waist and we plunge in to what is as yet to us a region of mystery — a northern virgin forest. Our guides precede us and occasionally the crash of their axes reveal to us the obstacles in our way.

Slowly and cautiously we thread our way upward, turning, now to the right, now suddenly to the left, now retracing our steps to seek a better path amongst the giant fir, spruce and birch trees that surround us on all sides. Now tripped by a sudden snag, and tumbling headlong into the downy mass, from which we are extracted by the legs and present a most ludicrous appearance to our laughing companions. Behind us come the dogs and driver, tumbling over the stumps and over each other, entangling their harness, barking, yelping with joy, or curling themselves amongst the brushwood, from which they are dragged, amidst the kicks and half muttered curses of their driver.

At length, after one hour's walking, we reach the summit, yet owing to the dense foliage we should not have believed so, had we not been assured by our guides. Panting and overheated, we throw ourselves down on the snow to take a short rest. Our guides profiting by the delay, open their "nunny bags" (large sealskin pouches) from which they draw forth a good lunch. The dogs are lying at our feet, apparently greatly interested in our proceedings. Suddenly a gigantic arctic hare dashes down the path and away go the dogs like wild fire, and the guides dropping all rush after them. Happily the dogs had not gone far before their harness became entangled in a tree, and when the guides reached the spot they found them in a heap, clawing and tearing each other most unmercifully.

We now commenced our downward course, catching through the foliage, fleeting glances of Canada Bay, flying across lakes; avernian shades, hidden in dark and gloomy forests. As we advanced, the forest became less dense, the marks of the woodman's axe became more frequent, and at length a break in the forest opens to view Canada Harbour, with its French rooms and fishermen's dwellings, its fields and cattle. From an abandoned hut, formerly the dwelling of men employed quarrying marble, we obtain an excellent view of the harbour beneath.

On the right the land rises almost perpendicular from the sea-shore to the height of about 500 feet. Directly beneath us and at the upper end of the harbour stretches a level plain, through which in summer a stream of sparkling water, well stocked with trout, meanders. One or two huts stand here. On our left is the settlement proper, consisting of four or five log cabins, stables and stages and French fishing-room. Around these huts are some primitive gardens and meadows, and behind the land gradually rises, showing here and there vast patches of excellent limestone, and on the distant summit the eye beholds the prominent fir.

Photo courtesy of Mrs. Anna (Hamlyn) McCarthy

Conche in the 1960s

We are now obliged to change our mode of conveyance, in order to cross Canada Bay. So we procure a large skiff. In this we placed our dogs and kometic. Our guides, together with a couple of inhabitants of Canada

Bay, man the oars, and we start. The wind was now blowing from the north-west, and out on the open bay it seemed to send the blood frozen back to our heart. We pass Englee Island at the mouth of the bay, and obtain a passing glimpse of its church and houses, and are told there are about 150 settlers residing there. Some of the houses appeared fine substantial construction, and two or three vessels at anchor in the harbour seemed to indicate a flourishing settlement.

We quit our boat at Boyd's Arm, and enter a perfect forest of wild balsams. After an hour's toilsome tramp upwards through the dense wood, we reach the summit of the mountain range that extends from Englee to Conche. Along this lies our course. The large trees have disappeared and in their place we find a few stunted firs, whose gnarled branches are twisted by the snow and ice into the most fantastic shapes. Scarcely do we see one of the trees above five feet high, but the trunks are thick and hard. It would require a strong arm and a sharp hatchet to fell them to the ground.

It had now begun to snow and the light drifts were scudding over the mountains. The cold was intense and we half smothered each other with snow to prevent being frost-bitten. A few miles distant is a solitary house in a small harbour called Bontiton; this we endeavoured to reach before the full force of the storm would set in. Our dogs careen madly through the blinding snow. The drifts become more and more dense, and just as we begin to lose courage, a glad yelp from our dogs is answered from a forest near at hand, tells us that we have passed the bleak barren highlands and will soon be in the shelter of the dense wood.

We enter the forest, pass quite a number of beam houses on our way, and finally fatigued and hungry we arrive at Bontiton. The shades of night were rapidly descending on the earth as we enter the solitary log-cabin. The shrieking of the tempest became louder, and the cracking of nails told of the intense frost.

A roaring fire is made in the large wood stove, and after placing the best food that his humble dwelling could afford before us, our kind host stretched himself on the floor before the fire. Gradually, one after another the guides follow his example, until the whole floor is covered with sleeping forms. One alone remains awake to replenish the fire, and in turn is relieved by another. Thus the weary night passed away, the tempest screeching fiercely without, the dogs uttering long mournful howls or moans, that would make one imagine that something unearthly was passing over the face of the earth, the nails cracking every moment with the sharp quick report of revolvers, the snoring of seven or eight sleeping forms, lit up by the unsteady glare of the fire, the roaring of the fire, the bending form of the solitary watcher "crooning" some mournful air. All this, and the knowledge that on this Christmas Eve morning we were many miles from the nearest house, fixed that night indelibly in my mind that it will never be forgotten.

Towards dawn, the storm began to abate, and about nine o'clock we started anew on our journey; but owing to the quantity of snow that had fallen during the night we were unable to use our kometic. About twelve o'clock the guides proceeded to cook dinner. They select a spot away from the trees, and cutting some dead branches succeed in lighting a blazing fire. Then they opened their nunny-bags, and in less time then it takes to describe, the tea kettle is singing on the fire. Couches of green branches are made for us, on which we stretch our weary limbs, and we imagine that the ancient

Romans, reclining on their perfumed couches, could not have enjoyed their banquets as we did enjoy our simple fare, stretched on sweet scented beds of fir and spruce.

Our meal over we start forth anew, and two hours later the bell tower of the Catholic Church of Conche breaks upon our view. We lose sight of it, we see it again between trees, and at length, climbing on a hill, the beautiful little village itself bursts upon our view, on the opposite side of the semi-circular harbour. The neat, white well-built cottages, the noise of hammer and saw, and the view of numerous men engaged at different works, proved beyond doubt, that the inhabitants were an industrious race. The pressing invitations that the guides received in all directions showed that the people were very hospitable, and the correctness with which they sang some airs, whilst at work, indicated culture that one would not expect in such an out-of-the-way place.

The next morning I was awakened from a profound sleep by the merry peals of the Christmas bell summoning us to early mass. On entering the pretty little church, I was surprised at the many signs of correct taste, shown in its decorations for the Christmas festivities. Delicate festoons of green boughs, in which variegated mosses were harmoniously blended, decorated the walls. Garlands of evergreens gracefully entwined the pillars, numerous chandeliers pendent from the ceiling, threw a blaze of light over the interior. On the Gospel side of the altar, a diminutive stable, thatched with branches, had been placed. In this was the crib, before which twinkled a number of tiny tapers throwing light on the image of the Divine Infant, and on a silver star suspended above the stable by an imperceptible thread.

Mass commences and it is the *Royal Mass of Durmont* that the choir sings. One of those simple Masses in Gregorian chant, which say more to the heart, and which excite more to piety, then the chief d'eoeuvres of modern art. Of course, beseiged as we were by King Frost, whose battalions were already hemming us in, on all sides, we could not but feel our isolation. After Mass, as I sat musing by my fire, a feeling of sadness engendered by my lonely position, crept over me, and I lived again in thought Christmases gone by, and familiar faces that I am destined never more to see, came crowding from their graves, laughing and living as they had laughed and lived in those happy Christmases of the past. Oh, Christmas! What memories do you revive, some gay, some sad, but alas, at each succeeding return of the day more faces come up from dreamland and haunt us with memories of long ago. As I mused and mused, I could not but help repeating over and over these beautiful lines of the Laureate:

> The time draws near the birth of Christ;
> The moon is hid, the night is still;
> A single church below the hill
> Is pealing, folded in the mist.
>
> A single peal of bells below,
> That wakens at this hour of rest
> A single murmur in the breast,
> That these are not the bells I know.
>
> Like strangers' voices here they sound,
> In lands where not a memory strays,
> Nor landmark breathes of other days,
> But is new unhallowed ground.

First Christmas at St. Thomas's Home, Villa Nova (1885)

by Father Michael Morris

Christmas memories! Christmas joys! Who is so poor that he cannot boast of one happy memory—even though a childish one—of this feast day of charity and peace to all men. Christmas memories! What a world of thought and feeling they can call up for us, even when we are but midway of life's pilgrimage. And surely if the poet's soul was vexed because a peasant could see in a yellow primrose "by the river bank" no more than a yellow primrose, may we not say he is a stranger in Christendom if the return of Christmas stirs no joyful and happy memory in his heart?

Christmas memories! How varied they are—gay and gladsome; aye and sometimes sad and sorrowful, because of the vanished faces and the vacant chairs at the Christmas fireside. But gladness is the prevailing and dominant note, and all memories of Christmas soul are tinged and softened by the thought of the Great Mystery evolved in Judea 2000 years ago.

Christmas memories! Yes how many of us could weave pleasant stories about them? "Well then give us some of your reminiscences of the Christmas - tide" that was your suggestion. Now at first I thought of giving your readers a breezy sketch of how we spent our Christmas holidays in the old school boy days. For I think the fun and frolic of these gay old mummering times, are now little better than traditions and memories. For our young generation, grown more aesthetic in their tastes, have eschewed many of the rough sports that in our days were inseparably associated with Christmas cheer.

Then I thought of recalling the memories of my first Christmas from home, when the knowledge had come to me that life had its duties and noble aims. When I began to believe that Christmas meant more than a time when mummers were to be decked out in their gay and garish colours, and snow palaces built in honour of old Santa Claus, that holidays with their snow ball-matches and sliding and skating and Christmas theatricals, were only accidentals in the celebration of this glad season. And just as the scenes and events in one's life will at a call, come trooping through the corridors of memory, in a kaleidoscopic order, some faint, some vivid; so with Christmas memories, here and there some stand out in bold relief. Your attention is especially called to the advent of the coming Christmas, as to a marked boundary in your career — a new chapter in your life — as a time for reflection, as an event to be remembered. And thus I recall as but yesterday, my first Christmas from home spent in the dear old Fatherland (Ireland).

Christmas Eve in our Irish Propaganda, was a high holiday and a busy feast day. Yet when we started for our long morning walk, and crossing the historic Volka Bridge, which stretched away down over the strand of Clontarf, I knew that some of us were thinking far more of home and the dear ones circling around the fireside, than of any historical association connected with the memorable battle-field on which we trod.

Well I knew that as we looked out that day over the troubled sea, and watched the silver flashing billows as they came rolling up through Dublin Bay, we felt that they come to us leaping and frisking over the Atlantic from our island Home; ay! and that the very sniff of the sea-breeze had come straight to us from Terra Nova, and we welcomed them as old friends bearing Christmas greetings.

And so if you will bear with me a little longer, I will pass over more than a decade of years to find myself in the year of grace 1885, a father with a great many little bright eyed boys looking up to me anxiously wondering how we would spent the first Christmas in our home in Villa Nova.

As the joyful days approached, you may be sure that we put our best efforts to make St. Thomas's Home as homelike as possible. We gathered bright ferns and pretty mosses and long wreaths of staghorn evergreen to decorate our little chapel, and lovingly we built the Christmas crib, that like a great Bible picture was to remind the little orphans of the desolation of the birth of the infant Saviour in the Rock Grotto of Bethlehem. But that was not all. Remembering that Christmas was not only a high religious festival, but also a gay and merry time; so when we had learned our Adeste and the other Christmas carols, we bethought of making some essays in juvenile theatricals in which a modified Bones and Pompey and a Barney Bralligan would figure prominently. How we succeeded you could easily tell from the roars of laughter that greeted the antics of the young play-actors.

But I was still doubtful as to the complete success of our first Christmas, for we had not grappled with the main difficulty — our commissariat department was not yet supplied.

Now hymns and songs and plays and magic lanterns are all very well in their way, they represent the nights and shadows of the merry time, but the innate essential idea ingrained in every boy's nature is that Christmas is a time when plum-pudding and pie and unmeasured quantities of sweet bread are to be had for the asking, and when the Christmas dinner is nothing without the savory *piece de resistance*, the traditional fat goose to crown the table.

Now I had set my mind on carving a goose for the boys on Christmas Day, and maybe I hoped to see it flanked with a couple of knightly surloins of beef and perchance a lordly turkey. Yet when we held a cabinet meeting, and I as Chancellor of the Exchequer showed our balance sheet and the bills due at Christmas, the proposition in *re the* turkey-goose question was rejected *ne. con.*

What! Was it possible that after all old Scrooge was right, and that "Christmas time was only for paying bills without money — a time for balancing your books and having every item in 'em presented dead against you." However we had another meeting on Christmas Eve to reconsider the question; the debate ran high. I felt like throwing up the seals of office and resigning or reconstructing the cabinet, when we heard the morning train slowing into the station at Villa Nova, and in a few minutes a couple of messengers ran in breathless to say there were ever so many parcels for us, including a fat goose. "And please Father," says one little fellow no bigger than Tiny Tim, "I think I smelled apples in a big box." Ah, but then the fun commenced. A detachment of the boys, on hearing the good news, started for the station, and I think the charge of the Light Brigade was slow going compared to the lightening speed in which they covered the ground. And sure enough there were the parcels and the goose in all its glory.

I could hardly count all the good things. Mrs. A. B. and C. sent such boxes of nice things, and would you believe it, before we came to the bottom of the first one out popped a beautiful sugared ham. Lady X apologized for the turkey not being up to the mark, though, when we weighed it, one of the boys said "he was afraid 'twas a fib she told, 'cause he never see the like of it before." Two little girls, I think they belonged to Bo Peep's merry crew, sent such a parcel of figs and currants; the pretty misses —, ever so many cakes nearly as nice as Lash's, not to talk of sweets and apples and oranges, and, to crown all, such a pretty letter, and all in round hand, too, from my little friend Gerald containing a crisp five pound note,

> To buy sugar and spice, and everything nice
> for the little boys at Villa Nova.

Well hadn't we such fun? Such a Christmas Day! How the little boys' hearts as they sang *Adeste Fideles*, and how thoughtful they looked when they were reminded that all the gifts sent to the poor and the little orphans at the holy Christmas time, are in memory of that Christmas night, twice 900 years ago, when the Holy Mother and the dear St. Joseph knocked at the doors in Bethlehem and sought in vain for shelter for themselves and the Divine Child.

Yes, for certain we did full justice to our Christmas gifts, and I know that before the day was half over we were after spoiling the juicy quarter of beef that Captain _____ so thoughtfully sent us. As for plum pudding and all the other accessories; well our good superintendent, who is not inclined to exaggerate, gave as his opinion that the bishop or the governor, or the biggest merchant of the city, ay, or even the Lord Mayor of London, couldn't sit down to a better dinner, or if they could, he defied them to have as good appetites. And so say we all.

* * *

A knock at the door! Why, bless my heart, I think I have been napping. I suppose tired out after all our fun and frolic on Christmas Day. "Christmas Day!" says the prosy superintendent: "Glad I am that we are within two or three days of it yet, so far you have not decided on what we are to have for the boys on that feast-day." And so it was only a dream; and the boys looking so disappointed when I described the grand time I dreamed of. "But please, Father," says one little fellow, "don't fret for I dreamed the other night of figs and bullseyes, and the next day I got apples."

Well who knows? There is plenty of time for the parcels to turn up, and so my dream be out. But anyway we are all of the opinion that whoever helps to make the dream a reality will deserve to be as happy as poor old Scrooge was when he bought on Christmas morning the famous turkey for Bob Cratchett's family. And so we wish you all a Happy Christmas.

(Villa Nova, December 22, 1885.)

Memories of Christmas in an Outharbour (1887)

by Mary J. Lynch

Perhaps there is no place in the world where Christmas is more eagerly looked forward to than in an outharbour. For months preceding there is nothing else talked of but anticipation and conjectures of what that great time will bring forth. All other topics are secondary to that of Christmas Day and Christmas doings, never forgetting to add a word now and then, of what transpired at that time last year. Well then, all comparisons being duly made, and necessary allowances being thrown in, it is decided, mentally or otherwise, that Christmas will bring forth better cheer this year than ever, and preparations go on accordingly. Of course I speak of those outports where the fishermen and planters having put through a good summer's work, and thriftily disposed of their hard earnings, are well prepared to meet the wants of the opening winter in even its sternest moods. As for those who have had bad voyages on our beloved shores, there it is otherwise. Christmas for them, indeed, must bear sad interest, especially where the piteous faces of little children are not gladded and dimpled as they ought to be, at this festive season. But even for those, our struggling ones, there is strong hope. When agriculture, now so happily awakened, shall have opened its giant mouth, and with its great iron tongue, the plow; and its Sampson's teeth, the harrows, shall have proclaimed its sway throughout the length and breadth of the land, in that not remote time, I trust there will dawn no more such unhappy Christmases as is now the misfortune of some few of our poor countrymen to witness.

Christmas at Hopedale, Labrador (1892)

by Samuel King Hullon

Of course we had Christmas in Labrador; and the people called the day by its right name, what is more. "Jesub Inulervia" (Jesus's Birthday) was their name for the Day; for on Christmas Day their rejoicing was centred on the day when the Saviour Christ the Lord was born in Bethlehem.

Of the ordinary jollification and present giving, which we in the homeland associate with Christmas, we saw nothing; and yet the day was a day of rejoicing and happiness. All the families tried to be home from their sealing camps for Christmas. Up to midday and later, on Christmas Eve the sledges kept coming; for the children you may guess, were urging their parents to be "home" in good time, because at four o'clock in the afternoon was the Children's Special Christmas Service. So dogs were urged on with greater efforts; and the village was full of excitement as the cry of "Kemmutsit" (a sledge) arose, and the first one and then another family came bumping over the rough beach-ice just in time.

Inside the church all was warmth and brightness. A lighted Christmas tree stood in the centre aisle. In front of the missionary's table, a fire roared in the stove and the backless benches were crowded from end to end.

In the front rows sat the children; boys one side, girls on the other, with faces washed and shining, and with black hair brushed to sleekness. All had clean white smocks; the boys had their sealskin boots neatly tied below the knee with braid—nothing slipshod about Christmas Eve service—and every girl had a nice new hair ribbon. They were excited.

Of course they must sing; they had a little hymn of their own, set to a pretty little tune:

"Come, children, come to the manager,"

Only of course the words were Eskimo and began:

"Sorrutsit kaititse,"

and went on with a lot of "k's" and "t's."

But before they sang their hymn, there was the reading of the lovely Christmas story; about the shepherds who watched over their flocks by night and about the Baby in the manger among the cattle, because there was no room for the tired travellers in the inn.

The missionary prayed, and the choir sang an anthem, and the stove cracked in the quiet moments and the air grew hotter by reason of the crowd.

After that the great moment, for the children especially, but for everybody else as well, arrived. The door from the missionary's vestry opened, and chapel-servants came in carrying trays. Trays loaded with lighted candles and each candle stuck in a white turnip. Now a turnip is as great a treat , and more of a treat, perhaps to an Eskimo child, as an orange or an apple at Christmas-time in England; and then, you see there are no oranges and apples in Labrador, but the missionary manages to save some turnips for Christmas out of the garden stock. With great decorum the stately chapel-servants handed round the turnips till each little pair of childish hands was holding one. The organist then struck up the tune and the children sang their Christmas hymn.

After another hymn, sung right lustily by the whole congregation, the service was over. It was already dark; five o'clock on Christmas Eve, and some of the children managed to keep their little candles alight as they went homeward. We loved to watch the flicker as they made their way along. Some of the older women had lanterns, because they were not quite as sure-footed on the slippery snow as they used to be.

Silence fell; the lamps in the church were put out; the last of the lanterns disappeared in the distance; the people had gone home—home to decorate their own little Christmas trees.

The brass band woke us up on Christmas morning; we were in church by nine o'clock for the special Christmas Prayer Meeting. Then we went home for half-an-hour to meet again at ten for the Christmas sermon.

Later in the day the children assembled again and this time all eyes were on the vestry, for Father Christmas was coming. At just the right moment the door opened, and in came the well-known figure of picture and story—red and furry gown, long white beard and a sack of presents.

Along the rows of children he went, handing a little parcel to each—and friends in England may rejoice at this happy way of distributing the gifts they have sent.

The children gaze in some little awe at the portly bearded figure. Some of them forgot to say their "nakomek" (thank you) as they clutch the parcel which he hands to them, just as children in England sometimes forget under similar circumstances! Who is Father Christmas? Who is he? Who can it be? Perrett has kept the secret well. It is not himself, for he is there presiding over this happy scene and seated smiling behind the missionary's table. No, reader I cannot tell you for I do not know myself. When I ask Perrett, he just laughed in his hearty way and left me wondering.

Hopedale in 1951

Surely one of the most lovely things in the world is to make little children happy. Such was our Eskimo Christmas; a time of remembering the birth of Jesus and of thanking God for the coming of the Saviour Christ the Lord.

Memories of Christmas (1893)

by John Maclay Byrne

Christmas Eve, Boston 1893

Christmas Eve, accompanied by a storm of unusual severity. The wind, beginning with a low crooning sound, gradually increases to a furious shriek, and then dropping into a despairing moan—like the cry of a human being from whom all hope has fled—goes rushing along dark and gloomy streets and forbidden looking courts and alleys, driving before it, in its mad rush, millions of blinding white snowflakes, and causing the ramshackle tenements to rock and sway on their uneven foundations. Snow, hail, and sleet mingle together, covering the outside world, pattering and dashing against the window panes, as if jealous of the warmth and comfort displayed through their dripping surfaces. It is a night that serves to heighten one's appreciation for the comforts of one's fireside, and settling back in the depths of my cosy arm chair I listen to the howling of the storm and feel thankful that "my lot has fallen in pleasant places," while so many others, more deserving than I have not whereon to lay their heads.

The fire-light dances upon the walls, causing fantastic shadows to flit to and fro, and the flickering embers in the grate seem, to my contemplative mind, to form pictures of scenes that are now almost forgotten memories. Suddenly the storm ceases for a moment and the sound of bells, ushering in the Christmas morn, come floating in upon the frosty air; the mellow tones, which seem to echo the joyous refrain of a Celestial choir pour in with an indescribable sweetness into my soul, and there steals over my senses, like the dawn of a summer day over the rugged mountain tops, a feeling of ecstasy, tinged with sadness, which causes unwilling tears to spring to my eyes. Hosts of memories rise up before me and pass in familiar review; memories of a past, dim and almost forgotten in the hurly burly of a life passed in a great busy city; memories of Christmas time and Christmas scenes in another land—a land made holy to me by happy associations and boyish delights; memories of early friends now scattered by the relentless hand of time; some, like myself, finding a home under a foreign sky, and others silently resting beneath the snow-covered sods of Belvedere.

Memories of Christmas in St. John's

With my mind filled with such pictures I fall asleep and dream. Once again I have passed through the sheltering gate which guards the entrance to our dear old town, and stand upon the sacred soil of home. Oh! How my heart pulsates with a new-found joy as each familiar scene bursts upon my hungry and delighted view. It is Christmas time; the shops are in a blaze of glory, with windows filled with toys and gifts of almost every description; miniature pyramids and mountains of the most tempting delicacies, festooned with wreaths of evergreen holly and mistletoe; Christmas cakes of extraordinary size and sugar workmanship; Christmas geese, each one as fat and tempting as ever Mrs.

Cratchit's was; Christmas turkeys, larger and fatter than Scrooge's, all signalize the presence of that greatest of Christian festivities. But best of all are the hearty Christmas greetings amongst the jovial, happy crowds, as they stagger along under the weight of a mighty goose or a load of presents for the expectant little ones at home.

Each face I see is beaming with happiness and good will. Within doors all is bustle and preparation, and many of the scenes are worthy of a touch from the magic brush of the great master, whose Christmas portraits we all know and love so well. A huge fire burns in the open grate, shedding a cheerful glow over the room, and sending the sparks crackling and roaring up the chimney, bidding defiance to Jack Frost. Seated in an old fashioned rocker before the fire, calmly enjoying his pipe, and taking an occasional sip from a glass of something hot, sweet and strong, is the master of the house, a picture of enviable contentment. The good wife with her sleeves rolled up on her bare honest arms is busily stuffing the morrow's goose, whilst gathered around the table, which is generously laden with the constituents necessary for a Christmas dinner, are the younger members of the household, interestedly watching the delightful preparations, and, when opportunity offers, purloining some of the contents of the well-filled plates. When at last the final stitch is put in the goose, and the pudding, with its bloated, jolly face, is sewed in its immaculate white cloth, the youngsters are led away to bed, to dream of the well-filled stockings hanging in the chimney corner.

Now the table is set with jugs, glasses, and decanters, and plates of "sweet bread," apples and oranges, and old friends drop in with "A Merry Christmas" to sit up the night. They gather round the table and the fire — a happy healthy crowd — and, as I look into their ruddy, smiling faces, it seems as if the angel of peace had touched all present with his magic wand, smoothing out the furrows of care from the brows of the aged, and driving from every heart the germs of selfishness and ill-will. Every new arrival is greeted with "A Merry Christmas" and a hearty shake of the hand. Toasts are drunk, in steaming glasses of home-brewed punch to the memories of old times and old-time friends, and when the dead are mentioned a pious "God Rest his Soul," with the answering "Amen" is heard from all present. Soon tongues are loosened, and the conversation becomes animated with native humour, which is never of a very low order. The old folks "swap" reminiscences and become young again, as they regale each other with yarns of old sealing days, and bewail the changes which have come over the good old times, when a trip to the ice-fields brought rich returns that amply repaid the hardships endured.

A fiddler of local renown is one of the company, and after several internal applications of punch, which seem to be as essential to the player as rosin to his bow, *The Banks of Newfoundland*, *Garry Owens* and all the old favourites are rattled off. One of the boys is prevailed upon to sing, but he modestly protests and pleads either a cold or that he "don't know no song." Finally after a deal of coaxing (and I think that bright eyed girl in the chimney corner had more to do with his consenting than all the others), he begins or rather prepares to begin. He coughs several times, smiles, and again faintly protests that he has a cold, but excuses being of no avail, he stretches out his legs to their full length, puts his hands in his trousers pockets, and throwing back his head, fixes his eyes on the ceiling and begins. His selection is not latest opera nor probably the earliest, but is a good old fashioned "Come all ye's," handed down from grandfather and father, each line terminating with a note of extraordinary duration. The voice of the singer may be a little out of order, but that is of slight consequence, as he makes up in volume and hearty enthusiasm what he may lack in tone. The ruthless critic is not present, and mistakes and break-downs are passed over with good humour.

Artwork of St. John's around 1860.

Christmas at King's Cove, Bonavista Bay (1900)

by J. T. Lawton & P. K. Devine

Christmastide was anticipated keenly by young and old. It was mummering time. Long before Christmas, considerable time was spent on designing costumes and fantastic rigs. Christmas Eve ushered in the mummering period, and for a whole fortnight, the night air was tortured by the inarticulate cries peculiar to "jannies." The mummers went around in groups of various numbers touring the village from one end to the other. There was a heroic folk-play brought by the Irish immigrants from the "Old Country" that used to be performed by young men during the Christmas holidays. The actors personated some of the great heroes of history, Napoleon Bonaparte, Alexander, Dr. Faustus, Sir Isaac Newton, St. George, St. Patrick. But times have changed. Today the tidy housewife will not admit nine or ten roughly shod boys on her red-and-white chequered canvas. In the olden days, the sanded floor could stand considerable traffic. The usual refreshments handed out to the mummers were sweet cake and a glass of peppermint.

King's Cove was always famous for the number of violinists. On Christmas Eve they paraded through the village — numbering sometimes a dozen violinists — with the accompaniment of drum, cymbals, triangle and tambourine. The drum was made from a sawed off flour barrel with goat skin heads. The cymbals were two pot covers. The triangle was a pair of tongs and the tambourine was a tinpan or metal tray. One Christmas Eve night, Stephen Ryan of Broad Cove played the tambourine. The night being chilly and his hands exposed, they lost their sensitiveness, and when the parade was over, his knuckles were a mass of mangled flesh and blood. The incident is trivial; but it shows the hilarious fervour of the amusements of the olden days in Old King's Cove.

One Christmas in Germany (1918)

by Captain Leo C. Murphy

The Christmas of 1918 spent with our troops on the Rhine has afforded us an object lesson of what the Yuletide spirit really means throughout the world. In Germany for instance, there is a nation peculiarly situated, a war power defeated in its objects, and a people learning a bitter lesson; but notwithstanding these conditions they made a real attempt to keep the Christmas festival. In the old market the tops of the fir trees were heaped for sale; fairy rain and glass decorations were displayed in the shops where foodstuffs were at an abnormal figure, and crowds were waiting near the few stores where sweets could be procured. In the evening in the smallest houses, the little fir-trees were illuminated and there was music, the children joining hands and singing in a circle. At the place where Lieut. Clouston and I were billeted, our host, a German professor of languages in a well known college, brought our orderly in to see this family gathering, and pointing to the children said in perfect English, "Thank goodness they do not know what war means."

The year fell sadly here, in spite of peace and freedom, so appalling has been the catastrophe, and so terrible the change from growing prosperity to want; but all the men in our regiment enjoyed special food, well cooked, and an extra issue of pudding, chocolates, tobacco, cigarettes, and beer and arrangements were also made to organize games, so that in addition to the educational classes, they should also enjoy football, basketball and other advantages. The Divisional concert party held two excellent entertainments on New Year's Day, and the Regimental Fife and Drum Band played out 1918 and welcomed 1919 with a flourish that awakened the streets of the old German village where we are in barracks.

Memories of a Christmas Eve Long Ago (1921)

by Tim Shannahan

There are many sorrows to be endured going through life and there are many joys that make up for them. But I know of no greater sorrow than that experienced by the boy who loses his last ten cent piece on the wheel of fortune on Christmas Eve Night. He hopes to win a fine fat goose or a Christmas cake. He slips in among the crowd and purchases his ticket, the wheel spins and he loses. He has one more ten cent piece and he feels there many be better luck in store for him so he tries again. Away goes the wheel, "Look out for your numbers" is shouted while his eyes are riveted on the numbers as they spin around. The proprietor yells out "fifty-four, who has fifty-four?" and a cute looking man with a parcel under his arm walked through the crowd and carried off the "fine fat goose."

This was my experience when I was a lad on a Christmas Eve of long ago, and as I left in the blues, almost blue enough to cry and was about to quit the place, when a man came forward and slipped another ten cents piece in my hand saying, "have another try."

I did not know that man, but my heart went out to him for he gave me a taste of joy that no words can describe. With the tenner of course I bought the ticket and with that ticket I won the "fine, fat goose."

Who is he that won a goose for the first time and forgets the incident? He may forget who his godfather was, but never will he forget winning his first goose. No one could feel prouder, no one could be more elated than I as I almost ran from the store, never halting 'till I reached home with my prize. Halfway through the door I shouted to those inside the gladsome news that I had won a goose. My joy was participated in by all at home and soon the news got round the neighbourhood that I had won a goose, and before you could say "Jack Robinson" a dozen neighbours had arrived all proclaiming in strongest terms that it was the "finest goose they saw in a long time."

When the excitement was at its height some of the women asked me how I won it, and I up and told them of my losing my last ten cent piece and how a kind hearted man came to my assistance and bought a ticket for me. My dear old mother was smiling with delight as she listened to me relating my experience, and as I finished I will never forget her words. "Well," she said, "as we have a goose for our Christmas dinner, and as that man was so kind to you, if you take my advice you will give that goose to poor Mrs. Blank who lives over in the lane for her Christmas dinner." Honestly I hated to do it, but with some coaxing and promises of reward, I took the blooming bird over to our poor neighbour. I'll never think of half the prayers Mrs. Blank showered on me, nor will I forget the loud way she bawled out to her husband to come and see what had arrived. And although I hated to part with my goose at the start, to tell you the truth, I now feel that I was repaid for my generosity.

This is only a simple little story, but don't you think it conveys a lesson to us to treat boys generously? That man who stood the ticket for me gave a lot of pleasure to a lot of people. Today he is a prosperous business man in our own city and the kindness he showed me on that Christmas Eve, he has shown in a greater degree through life. We should remember that boys remember little acts of kindness; they seldom forget them.

Will our acts of kindness to the newsboy, the errand boy, and the cross sweeper, during the Festive Season be such as to cause those lads to remember them at Christmas in years to come?

Christmas on the S.S. *Baccalieu*
(1943)

by Alice Lannon

In 1943, I was attending St. Bride's College, Littledale in St. John's. "Littledale," as the college was known, was a boarding school for girls run by the Sisters of Mercy.

My father had decided that I should stay in St. John's for Christmas as the schedule of the S.S. *Baccalieu* didn't fit too well for my Christmas holidays. We got our Christmas holidays on December 15th and I went as planned to my brother Tom's boarding house on Field Street. The good sisters thought that my brother was married and living in town. I never told them that, they had just assumed it when I said I was spending Christmas with my brother. Had they known it was a regular boarding house with a number of male boarders I'm sure they would have kept me at the college.

Tom's boarding house on Field Street was run by two unmarried ladies, Lillian and Annie Sexton. They made me very welcome and the home cooked meals were a treat after nearly four months of boarding school food. As well they took me with them when they went downtown to Water Street to do their Christmas shopping. The buses at this time were always crowded with American and Canadian servicemen who were always ready to flirt a bit with the girls.

Water Street was a place of Christmas delight with all the stores decorated with bright coloured lights, and in one store there was a life-size mechanical Santa Claus playing a piano in the store window. The streets were thronged with busy shoppers, and the air was filled with the jingling of the bells on the horses as they went along the street with carts filled with packages, groceries and coal. The jingling bells were music to my ears and helped to make Water Street a place of magical fascination for me.

Two days before Christmas there was a soft snow falling outside and I was sitting by the window looking out when my brother Tom came in the room. I was thinking of home and he saw tears in my eyes. He didn't say anything, but he knew I was feeling homesick. The next day he went down to the railway station and bought me a return ticket to Terrenceville on the S.S. *Baccalieu*.

When he gave me the ticket, I said, "but I'll be late getting back to school." "It doesn't really matter," he said, "you'll only be a day or two late or at worst a week and you won't miss out." I was so overjoyed I didn't know how to thank him. Not only would I be home for part of Christmas, but I was also going to get a trip on the coastal boat which would be a special holiday in itself.

On Christmas Day I went with Tom to the High Mass at the Cathedral (Basilica) and the choir sang the beautiful old hymns in Latin. Lillian cooked a lovely Christmas dinner. All the boarders, except Tom, had gone home for Christmas, but a number of Lillian and Annie's friends from the South coast came in.

The morning of Boxing Day I was up early for I had to be at the railway station by nine o'clock to catch the train to Argentia to join up with the S.S. *Baccalieu*. It was spilling rain and Tom tried his best to get a taxi, but had no luck. It was war time and the taxi business was booming. Tom finally gave up trying and said "I guess we'll have to walk." Luckily the rain had now slacked off to a drizzle when we set out for the railway station.

However, just as we got to Freshwater Road the rain started to pour again. Then, a big Canadian Navy truck stopped and the driver asked if we wanted a lift. We got aboard and told him we were going to the railway station. On the way there we got talking and it turned out he had been born in St. Jacques and grown up there, but had moved away when we were little. He knew our parents very well. He even told Tom he would wait for him to get me settled away and give him a ride back. Both Tom and I felt that luck was with us that day.

The ride to Argentia was an interesting one. The train was crowded with sailors and soldiers going home on leave to the South Coast. There was music and singing which helped to pass away the time as the old "Newfie Bullet" chugged along the rails towards her destination. We arrived at Argentina about 1 p.m. in a storm of wind and wet snow and boarded the S.S. *Baccalieu*.

All the passengers gathered in the lounge and waited until the purser had taken our tickets and then the stewardess assigned me a stateroom which I was to share with three other young girls. When we were settled away, the stewardess came in and read the "Riot Act" saying we were to behave ourselves and she wouldn't tolerate any nonsense or carrying on late at night.

The stateroom had four bunks, two upper and two lower. I volunteered to take one of the top bunks near the porthole. But the porthole was locked and blacked out because of the war. We had a sink, but the bathroom was outside and served a number of cabins.

Because of the strong winds and a wartime rule that the ship did not travel at night, we stayed in Argentia until the next morning. The father of one of the girls in my cabin worked on the Argentia Naval Base and he came and sponsored us ashore. We went to the Newfoundland Club. Here a lot of American service-men flirted with us and bought us soft drinks and bars. They offered to escort us back to the coastal boat. Two girls accepted but another girl and myself declined. The warnings of the good sisters about the dangers of trust-ing strange men was too fresh in our minds.

We sailed right after breakfast the next morning, and the ships pulled away from the dock to the singing of the *Old Rugged Cross* sung by some passengers from Grand Bank and Fortune. There was always someone who could play the piano in the lounge and these passengers always sang a hymn as the ship left port. After the hymns came songs like the *White Cliffs of Dover, Until We Meet Again* and other wartime favourites.

Card playing was another favourite way of passing the time. The games began early in the morning and con-tinued late into the night. If you had a crib board and a deck of cards you were sure of an invitation to play. Crib and Whist and Forty-Fives and Auction or One Hundred and Twenty as it was better known were all played. There was also poker games but these usually took place in the Smoke Room on the Upper Deck. Between meals you were allowed to play in the Dining Saloon.

The Dining Saloon had about twelve tables; some seated four persons, others six. It was a great honour to be asked to sit at the Captain's table. Once when I dined at the Captain's Table, Captain Hounsel, when the meal was finished, turned to me and said, "Now I'll beat you at a game of crib, Young McCarthy." I felt honoured but a bit scared to play with the captain.

The steward cleared the table and brought a deck of cards and a crib board and we began. We were keeping fairly close to each other, but when we rounded the home stretch, the captain was about seven points ahead. I almost caught up to him on the next deal. It was my first count and when I looked at my cards I had the perfect twenty-nine point hand.

The stewards who were cleaning the tables were watching us and when one fellow saw my hand, the word spread to the galley and a number of them came out and while pretending to clean up were keeping a close eye on the game. Captain Hounsel had a good hand and felt he was going to win. When I put down my hand, all the stewards clapped and cheered. The captain wasn't a gracious loser. With a scowl he took his hat from the hook behind his chair and went out the door. However, he did congratulate me on my good luck the next time I sat at his table. I was a celebrity for a day as the word spread that Alice had beaten the "Old Man" at crib. Only once or twice in all the following years have I ever seen the twenty-nine point hand again.

Our first port of call on the outward voyage was Marystown. We had a lot of freight to unload here, including a lot of flour and sugar sacks. As it rained rather heavily there was a delay in unloading the freight and we spent two days and two nights in that port, but a few of the passengers went ashore.

Then, it was on to St. Lawrence where the rainy weather again delayed us. There was dance and soup supper in the Parish Hall so a lot of us went to the dance and had a grand time. At that time St. Lawrence was a thriving mining town and well lit up for Christmas. There was a restaurant called the "Miner's Inn" and we visited there to buy cokes and listen to the jukebox.

While in St. Lawrence I was invited by a young nurse whom I had made friends with to go visit Mrs. Mary Slaney, a former patient of hers at St. Clare's. Mrs. Slaney welcomed us to her home and served us wine and delicious fruit cake and even gave us some cake to take back to the ship. Her home was beautifully decorated with a large Christmas tree in her front window with blinking lights that lit up her front steps. We even got to hold the new baby that my nurse friend had helped deliver just one month before.

Our next port of call was Grand Bank and again the town was all lit up with Christmas lights winking and blinking in many of the houses. As it was now New Year's Eve, the passengers decided to have a dance to celebrate the passing of the old year and welcome the new. The deck area between the companionway and the smoke room was chosen as the dance floor. We had an accordion player among us and he supplied the music. The dance lasted well on into the early morning hours and all hands had a marvellous time.

We left Grand Bank on New Year's Day for Bay L'Argent, but a sudden storm came up and Captain Hounsel decided to take shelter in St. Jacques Harbour on the other side of the Fortune Bay. It was a pretty rough crossing and there were very few besides myself who turned out for breakfast that morning. This was the only time I saw the sides on each table used to keep the dishes from sliding off the table.

As we entered St. Jacques Harbour I went out on deck to look at my old hometown. Our house was no longer standing, but the church and the school stood out against the grey sky. The salt spray hitting my face hid the tears in my eyes as a wave of nostalgia from the past swept over me. Then, I brushed them away and went in to partake of my first turkey dinner ever. It was a traditional turkey dinner with all the trimmings and there was a glass of wine at each place setting. Wishes of "Happy New Year" were exchanged between all the diners.

A Green Christmas in St. Jacques, Fortune Bay.

Photo courtesy of late Maurice Burke

The storm blew out around 3 p.m. and we got underway for Bay L'Argent. We spent the night there and the next morning I went ashore in the mail boat at Terrenceville. It was January second and I had spent a full week on the S.S. *Baccalieu*. The return trip ticket had cost twenty dollars and meals were included. If the ticket had been below twenty dollars I would have had to pay for my meals, and that would have made for a very expensive trip.

It was good to be home and have a few days of Christmas celebration with my family. Then, I also had the pleasure of looking forward to the return trip on the coastal boat. I had about a week home and then the S.S. *Baccalieu* arrived on her inward voyage. The return voyage only took three days, and as the S.S. *Baccalieu* was going on dry dock for refit, we went all the way to St. John's. It was a Christmas at sea that I will never forget.

Photo courtesy of Joe Prim

S.S. *Baccalieu* stuck in the ice near Rate Point, Bay d'Espoir.

Memories of a Christmas Eve in St. Joseph's, St. Mary's Bay (1940s)

by Joseph Dobbin

Remember Christmas Eve when you were a youngster? There was a special feeling you had all day. Your spine tingled as you went about your chores. Of course looking back on that special time there were many good reasons for all that excitement.

It was the day the Christmas tree was put up. Remember all the decorations? There was the cardboard star for the top; your mother had cut it out of a shoe box and covered it with silver paper. There were glass figures of angels, snowmen and Santas which your father had brought home from the base in Argentia. There was the red and green rope which criss-crossed the branches. There were the icicles you had painstakingly cut from the "Orange Pekoe" tea packages. Finally there was the "Angel Hair" which sat underneath the ten or twelve Christmas cards which had been set on conspicuous places on the tree's outstretched arms. Remember how you stood back and admired your masterpiece—the most beautiful Christmas tree ever.

Surely you must also remember supper on Christmas Eve? Your mother would spread a pure white tablecloth on the large eating-room table. In the centre of this she would place a raised cake dish on which was majestically sitting the Christmas cake—mother's masterpiece! A dark fruit cake baked in the big iron pot and

flavoured with a mug of father's black Demerara rum —
sneaked from one of his precious bottles secured with
his "Liquor Book" for Christmas.

Photo courtesy of Joe Dobbin

Christmas in St. Joseph's, St. Mary's Bay
(looking westward along St. Joseph's shore).

What an enjoyable meal supper would be! There'd
be baked fish with lots of onions, rashers and stuffing,
vegetables from your fall harvest followed by slices of
dark fruit cake and cups of strong tea.

After supper your father would go upstairs to "rag-
up." In a little while he'd be in his usual spot, the chair
at the end of the kitchen table, smoking quietly on his
pipe. Can't you see him now? A kindly man in his white
starched shirt and blue serge pants. His eyes would have
a special sparkle tonight and every so often he'd
exclaim, "Listen, isn't that bells I hear? Or I believe I

heard reindeer. I expect that Santa's gone along now."
What pleasant words for little ears!

Chistmas at the Dobbin House, St. Joseph's, St. Mary's Bay. Pictured is Joe Dobbin waltzing with Rose and Samantha and her dolly.

Around seven o'clock your neighbours would come in to while away the few hours before Midnight Mass. You'd listen to Christmas songs on the radio, revel in the memories of long ago, have a visit from the Mummers and entertain a few who came to have a nip of your father's Christmas cheer.

Finally it was time to go to Midnight Mass. You would be greatly excited about this because it was a "first" for you. You'd bundle up in your woolens and walk the mile or two to church. What a thrill it was to be out so late on a frosty night!

When you arrived at church you'd be awestruck by its splendour; warm and inviting, the smell of evergreens, the rows of pews filled with friends and neighbours, the Christmas crib and the captivating strains of Mrs. Ryan's music for Midnight Mass.

Harken! Can't you hear the rich baritone of Kevin Gough in the *Adeste Fideles* or the soft cultured voice of Mildred Fagan in the "et incaratus est?"

With Mass finally at an end and Father Enright having given you your Christmas Box, you returned with great anticipation to your home, bed and surprises which would greet you on Christmas morning when you retrieved your woolen stocking from underneath the Christmas tree.

A Fogo Island Christmas (1952)

by Mike McCarthy

Although I am not a native of Fogo Island, I had the good fortune to spend Christmas 1951 in the towns of Fogo and New Year's 1952 in Tilting. Now, whenever the Christmas season rolls round I fondly remember my Fogo Island Christmas.

In the fall of 1951, I travelled by the old S.S. *Glenco* to Fogo to teach in Our Lady of the Snows School in Fogo. It was usually a three day voyage to Fogo, but on this trip the Honourable Gordon Bradley, newly appointed to the Canadian Senate, was introducing Jack Pickerskill to the voters of the District as his successor and it took nine days to get there.

In due course I arrived at Fogo and went ashore in the mailboat because it was too stormy to get to the wharf in Seal Cove. Here I had the good fortune to meet Maggie and Billy Butt with whom I boarded, and they provided me with a home away from home.

As the Christmas holidays drew near, I debated whether or not I would go home for Christmas. It would be a long and round-about journey to get to my hometown, Terrenceville, in Fortune Bay. A journey that involved travel by boat and train and car with the possibility that the road from Goobies to Terrenceville might be closed by a major snowfall. After much soul searching I accepted the invitation of Bill and Maggie Butt to spend the Christmas holidays with them. It turned out to be a Christmas I shall never forget.

The Christmas season began for me in early December when the students of Our Lady of the Snows School began to practice for the Christmas Concert to be held just before Christmas. There was the usual hustle and bustle of casting for who would play what parts in the plays, the choice of songs and recitations, and the folkdance that was always one of the most popular segments. When the teacher pressed too hard towards perfection, there were tears and threats of not taking part, but generally everything went well and by mid-December, we were just about ready to go on stage.

Then shortly before recess time on the morning of December 12, a knock came on the school door and when I opened it, a distinguished looking gentleman introduced himself as Mr. William Galgay of C.B.C. He told me they had come to Fogo to record a radio program of "Christmas in Fogo" to be broadcast on Christmas Day on the local C.B.C. network. They had been looking for a school concert as part of their program and had been directed to our school.

I told him we were putting on a concert for Christmas and agreed that he could record portions of it for his program. As the school had no electricity the C.B.C. technicians accompanying Mr. Galgay set up a portable generator and we were ready to record. They weren't interested in the dramatic skits, but the songs and recitations were recorded and the kids under the pressure of being heard across Newfoundland sang and recited in a way I hoped they would repeat on the night of our concert. The recording of our school's Christmas concert by the C.B.C. was I think the highlight event in our school for that year. Needless to say the concert was a grand success on the night we performed for the parents and helped us raise some much needed funds for the school.

Christmas holidays began on the day after the concert, and on Tib's Eve, December 23, I had my first Fogo Christmas celebration. It began at Captain Paddy Miller's house and ended at a little before dawn in a house in Backcove, where a feast of warmed-over turrs and good home-brew beer was a fitting close to a night of Christmas revelry. I prefer not to dwell on my early morning Christmas Eve hangover.

On Christmas Eve night I went with Maggie and Bill to Our Lady of the Snows Church and here the late Father (later Monsignor) Joseph O'Brien celebrated Midnight Mass. Father O'Brien was a devout priest and a gifted preacher and he brought an aura of the first Christmas in Bethlehem to that little church in Fogo that I shall never forget. There was also an amusing incident that showed the Christian charity and great forbearance of that gentle and good priest.

One of the parishioners, a good man, who always attended mass, obviously had a little too much to drink before coming to church. He went up to his accustomed place in a front pew, knelt down and in a rather loud voice began to recite his prayers. Even during the sermon his Paters and Aves went on, but it didn't seem to bother Father O'Brien who showed no signs of annoyance. On the way out one of the more prominent ladies of the congregation, annoyed by the loud prayers, said to the priest, "Father, you must have been disgusted by such behaviour?" His answer was a classic. "Not at all, not at all," he said, "sure how could a man do better than come to church on Christmas Eve and pray. I'm sure God understood."

After Mass it was back to the Butts' and a Christmas feast fit for a king, with good brandy to wash it down and an exchange of Christmas gifts. On Christmas morning we sat around the radio and waited for the C.B.C.'s Christmas broadcast. Eventually it came on and we all felt the kids of Our Lady of the Snows had contributed greatly to the program.

Christmas dinner was an absolute triumph with a plum pudding that was mouth watering awash in a marvellous brandy sauce. After dinner I visited with some friends and was plied with enough Christmas cheer to last me for a decade. There was one thing about the people of Fogo Island; a stranger in their midst was certainly made to feel welcome.

On Boxing night the mummering began. This was great fun and the reception varied from house to house as did the treats. One of our number had an accordion and if the answer to our "Any mummers 'llowed in?" was "yes" we would dance and talk mummer talk with the best of them. London Dock, home-brew, moonshine, spruce beer, Purity syrup, limejuice and even hot ginger wine were offered along with a variety of cakes and other sweets. Needless to say a good time was had by all.

On the night of December 27th, the young people hired the Star of the Sea Hall and we had a dance and ate and drank and played "forfeits" until the early hours of the morning. Christmas celebrations were the order of the day.

On December 29th, I received an invitation from Father O'Brien to spend a couple of days at his home in Tilting, another Fogo Island community. As the snow had held off and the road was still open to Tilting I was happy to accept his invitation. This meant that I would get to attend the parish New Year's "Time" in the Hall, as well as to enjoy the hospitality of the Tilting people.

In the parish house, Father O'Brien and his house-keeper Bride Maddox did everything to make a stranger welcome and introduced me to various people including Mr. Ron Burke and his wife, Rose, two of the most hos-pitable people I have ever met. Ron made the best home-brew I've ever tasted and he was a whiz at cards. They too made me very welcome and helped make my Christmas in Tilting a never to be forgotten event.

I should mention that at an earlier time, the guest room in the Tilting Parish House was supposed to have been haunted by an alien presence that defied every attempt to oust it. In fact, a former pastor had been so tormented by its presence, he had closed up the house and moved to other quarters. The house had been opened again some years later by another pastor and it seemed the alien presence had departed. This was the room I was to sleep in. I must confess that the first night I slept in the room I was more than a little uneasy, but nothing happened and for the rest of my visit I was totally at ease.

As in Fogo, mummering was a part of the Tilting Christmas celebration and again I took part. Dressed in an old suit belonging to Father O'Brien and with a rather grotesque mask I was able to pass muster. As in Fogo there was much lively banter, drinks and eats of many varieties, and all kinds of attempts to discover the iden-tity of the various mummers. Again, the mummering expeditions were a great success and added much to the Christmas festivities.

The New Year's "Time" in the Parish Hall was also an event to be remembered. Games of chance, dancing, and a delicious supper were the orders of the day. I was able to add a little diversity by telling fortunes with a deck of cards and helped raise a few dollars. I sat at a table with the cards and a gentleman of the community sat behind a screen next to me. As a prospective client approached, the gentleman would fill me in with a few details about the person, which I in turn read from the cards to the total amazement of the persons seeking to know their fortune.

Joe Kinsella, a native son of Tilting Harbour, who had taught in Our Lady of the Snows School at Fogo the year before, was home from University for Christmas and invited me to his home where I enjoyed the hospitality of Joe and his parents. Like all the people I met in Tilting they went out of their way to make sure that the stranger was made to feel welcome and made a part of their Christmas celebrations.

However, all good things must come to an end and on Old Christmas Day I returned to Fogo for the reopening of school on the following day. It's a long time since I spent that happy Christmas in Fogo and Tilting, but whenever the Christmas Season rolls round I remember again Maggie and Billy Butt and Father Joseph O'Brien and Bride Maddox and the other people of Fogo and Tilting who did so much to make my Christmas away from home a very happy one.

Newfoundland and Labrador

Christmas Tragedies

Christmas Night on the Cape Race Cliffs (1856)

by Frank Galgay & Mike McCarthy

On Christmas Day, 1856, The *Welsford*, a new 1380 ton vessel with a crew of twenty-six men, on her first trans-Atlantic voyage, was near the coast of southern Newfoundland. It was very foggy with a brisk breeze blowing and about 4:00 p.m. Captain Hatfield, believing he was past Cape Race, set the ship's course east by south by east and hoped for a quick passage across the Atlantic. Below deck, the off-duty crew were celebrating Christmas.

Under a single reefed topsail and top gallant sails, the ship was making about eight knots when without warning she suddenly struck with a violent shock that brought her foremast crashing to the deck. The men below scrambled on deck and joined their shipmates who had been on watch. Peering through the thick fog they could make out the dim outline of rugged cliffs towering above them. It was clear they had struck somewhere on the Southern Shore area of Newfoundland. Later they learned they had come to grief in Trepassey Bay, just a few miles below Cape Race.

In the initial panic following the crash, the ship's officers and the crew gathered together to decide what they should do. In the darkness and heavy fog it was impossible to judge how dangerous it would be to attempt a landing. To make matters worse the wind increased. The waves whipped into fury by the gale force winds which pounded against the rocks, making it impossible under such conditions to launch a boat. The ship however was wedged tightly between the rocks and although pounded by the surf did not seem in any danger of breaking up. Under these circumstances it was decided to wait for daylight before attempting to make a landing.

Then, later in the evening the wind changed direction and now Captain Hatfield's worst fears were realized. The ship began to pound against the rocks and in a short while her bottom gave way. This created a new danger for with her bottom gone the cargo of timber she was carrying broke free and began to crash against the ship's sides. As well, the surging timbers surrounding the ship now made it virtually impossible to launch a boat.

The end of the ship came quickly for even as the captain and crew debated their best course of action, there was a tremendous crashing sound and the ship's hull split into four parts. The men now had no choice but try and make it ashore or die like trapped animals on their doomed ship.

When the ship broke apart, the mate, Mr. William Journlay, and two other crew members, Malcolm Finlayson of Scotland and Thomas Hard of St. John's, were on the stern section. Realizing their imminent danger, they jumped from the ship and landed on a ledge of rock that cropped out from the steep, overhanging cliffs. The captain and the remainder of the crew on the other sections of the broken ship were not so fortunate. They too made it to the rocks, but the surf swept them off and they were crushed by the surging timbers.

The mate and his two companions crouched on their rocky ledge and listened in horror to the piteous screams of their doomed messmates as they went to their death. There was nothing they could do as the men were crushed by the surging timbers that surrounded the ship. The cries of the drowning men lasted for about a quarter of an hour; then, there was nothing but the shriek of the wind and the crashing of the waves. In a few hours a large ship had been reduced to matchwood and twenty-three men had gone to their death. The three survivors had no idea where they had landed; they could only huddle together on their rocky ledge and await the coming of dawn.

It was a Christmas Night that none of the three survivors would ever forget. Cold, wet and hungry they clung to their precarious perch on the ledge of rock that had saved their lives.

During the long hours of waiting they remembered the joys of Christmas with their families and of the families and friends of their dead shipmates celebrating the festive season, with no thoughts of the sorrow the coming days would bring to them.

At last after what seemed to them an eternity, the first rays of dawn began to lighten the eastern sky. With the coming of dawn, new hope filled their hearts and they were determined to scale the forbidding cliffs and find help in some near-by community.

When it was full daylight they looked around the area and called out in the hope that there might be other survivors. There were none and not even one bit of wreckage remained to show where the *Welsford* had gone down.

Having satisfied themselves that there were no survivors, they turned their attention to finding a way to scale the forbidding cliffs that towered over their rocky perch. There was no path and the sheer face of the cliffs struck terror into their hearts. However, there was no alternative; they had to scale the cliffs or die, so the desperate climb began. It was a slow and agonizing process, searching for footholds in the icy rocks and helping one another over the more difficult places. It took them a long time to reach the top, for one false step could spell disaster. But at last they made it, and happy but exhausted, threw themselves on the moss covered rocks to take stock of their situation.

They had no idea where they were or in what direction to travel. To make matters worse, the fog which had lifted earlier in the morning returned and visibility was reduced to nearly zero. In order to keep warm they wandered around trying to find some path or track that might lead them to human habitation, but found nothing. Cold, tired and hungry they were fast reaching the point of exhaustion when around midday the fog lifted again and they saw the tower of what proved to be Cape Race lighthouse about two miles away.

The sight of the lighthouse tower gave them new strength and they started off towards it, hoping the fog would not return until they had reached their destination. Although nearly exhausted they finally made it and knocked on the door of the lighthouse keeper's cottage.

It was a very surprised William Halley who answered the knock on his door, for visitors to Cape Race lighthouse at this time of the year were few and far between. However, he welcomed the survivors of the *Welsford*, and in a few minutes his wife was preparing food for the starving men. It was a novel experience for Halley and his wife to hear at first hand the story of a dreadful sea disaster for Halley was the first lighthouse keeper at Cape Race and he and his wife had only taken up residence there the previous summer. It was however a tale that Halley and his successors would hear time and time again in the succeeding years.

When the needs of the survivors had been met, the news of the loss of the *Welsford* and the names of the only three survivors was telegraphed to St. John's, over the recently installed telegraph line. The story of the wreck of the *Welsford* was printed in the 1857 New Year's edition of the *Newfoundlander*.

For two days the three survivors enjoyed the Christmas hospitality of the Halley's, where they were treated with every kindness and consideration. Then, Mr. Halley took them to Trepassey where they found passage on a ship to St. John's.

Lighthouse at Cape Race.

Author's Collection

A Gull Island Christmas Tragedy (1867)

by Frank Galgay & Mike McCarthy

On the morning of December 6th, 1867, the brigantine, *Queen of Swansea* left St. John's with a load of general cargo, the Christmas mail and a number of passengers for the Union Mine at Tilt Cove, Notre Dame Bay, Newfoundland.

The vessel was under the command of Captain John Owens, a native of Wales, and carried besides her regular crew of seven Cornish seamen, a local pilot, Patrick Duggan, a druggist, Felix Dowsley, who was to serve as medical officer at the Tilt Cove Mine, and William Hoskins and his sister who had come from Wales to spend Christmas with their father, the manager of the Tilt Cove Mine, and four other passengers.

Shortly after the *Queen of Swansea* sailed from St. John's, a terrible storm came on. Some weeks later, Patrick Duggan's trunk and some other wreckage from the "Queen" washed ashore near Twillingate. Everyone believed that the vessel had foundered with all souls lost.

It was not until the following April that there was further news of the ill-fated ship and a story of suffering and slow death was revealed which horrified and shocked the Newfoundland public. The story of the fate of the *Queen of Swansea* only became known when Captain Mark Rowsell of Leading Tickles, returning from a sealing voyage, became becalmed near Gull Island; a steep, barren, granite rock that rises out of the sea a few miles off Cape John.

While the ship was becalmed two sealers from Captain Mark's vessel launched a boat to go bird hunting. Near a deep gulch in the rock they shot and wounded a bird that flew to the top of the rock before falling. Not wanting to lose their kill, and the seas being dead calm, the two men entered the gulch with the intention of scrambling up the rocks to find the bird they had shot. On entering the gulch they saw a number of ropes dangling from a rocky ledge, about half way up the cliff. Intrigued, the two men climbed to the ledge and found a number of bodies frozen together under a piece of sail canvas and at some distance from the other bodies, two human skeletons. They immediately climbed down to their boat and brought the news of their grisly find to Captain Rowsell.

Captain Rowsell came back with them and when he examined the bodies knew that they were some of the missing passengers and crew of the *Queen of Swansea*. Leaving everything as it was, he sailed to Tilt Cove and asked for volunteers to go with him and his men to bring the bodies ashore. Patrick Mullowney, a brother-in-law to Duggan, the pilot, and Mr. Gill who was a coroner, along with a number of other Tilt Cove men returned to Gull Island with Captain Rowsell. They brought axes, crowbars and some rough coffins.

The party, under the direction of Mr. Gill and Captain Rowsell, removed the bodies and brought them to Tilt Cove. The authorities at St. John's were then notified of the tragic discovery. In the pockets of several of the dead men were notes and letters that told vividly of the hunger and pain and desperation of these victims of the sea.

In the pocket of Captain Owens was a short account of the disaster that had befallen them. Captain Owens wrote:

> The *Queen of Swansea* got on the rock of Gull Island, Cape John, Newfoundland in lat. 49 degrees 59 min and long. 55 degrees 11 min W, or thereabouts, on 12th, December, 1867. Consisting on board, altogether seven hands of crew and the master, which was eight in number of the ship's company, and six passengers and a pilot—two of the passengers being female altogether fifteen on board. The captain and mate and seven men and two females landed on Gull Island by means of a rope at 6:00 A.M., on the 12th of December, 1867, just as we stood, neither bread nor eatables nor clothes. Boatswain, pilot and one of the ship's crew went away with the ship, and a married man, (Power) who was one of the passengers. All these four perished with the ship. This is written on the island after landing, by me.
>
> (Signed) John Owens
> Master, *Queen of Swansea.*

In the pocket of Felix Dowsley's coat were found three letters to his wife which graphically described the horror they endured until death released them from their agony. The first letter was dated December 17, 1867, five days after they had been shipwrecked.

> Gull Island, off Cape John
> Tuesday, Dec. 17, 1867

My Darling Margaret:

As you are aware, we left St. John's on Tuesday morning, the 6th inst. On the evening of that day a dreadful gale came on, which lasted about two or three days. We were driven off about 160 miles to sea. I thought every moment the vessel would be upset or swamped, but it appears she was spared a little longer for a similar fate. We ran into a gulch on the island on the morning of Tuesday, the 12 inst., about 6:00 A.M., when the sea was raging and running mountains high. She only remained there ten or fifteen minutes, which was not sufficient time for all hands to save themselves. All were saved with the exception of two of the crew, Duggan, the pilot and Mullowney's stepbrother. We were dragged up the cliff by means of a rope tied around our waists. Not one of us saved a single thing but as we stood, not even a bit of bread; this is our fifth day, and we have not had a bit or sup, not even a drink of water, there being no such thing on the island. It is void of every-thing that would give us comfort. It is so barren and black that we cannot get wood to make a fire to warm us. Our bed is the cold rocks, with a piece of canvas, full of mud to cover us. You may fancy what my sufferings are and have been. You know I was never very strong or robust. My feet are all swollen and I am getting very weak. I expect that if Providence does not send a vessel along this way to-day or tomorrow, at the fartherest, some of us will be no more, and I fear I shall be the first victim, if so you will not have the gratification of getting my body as they will make use of it for food. I am famishing with the thirst. I would give all the money that I took with me for one drink of water. If I had plenty of water I know I should live much longer. I feel a dreadful feverish thirst, and no means of relieving it. Did I ever think my life would end in this way, to be cast away on a barren rock in the middle of the ocean, and there to perish with cold, hunger and thirst and my bones to be bleached by the winter's frost and the summer's sun and be food for the wild fowls. Is it not sad to think of this, and such a little thing would save us! We are only eight miles from Shoe Cove, where we would be received with open arms. Now, my darling Margaret, as I plainly see that in a few hours I must appear before my God, I wish to say a few words about your future prospects. {Here Mr. Dowsley gave some private and personal information to his wife and then concluded with a last request should his remains be found}.

Embrace my darling children and tell them to be obliging and kind to each other, for without this they cannot hope to prosper. Tell them their unfortunate father leaves them his blessing. Should our fate be known before the spring, if.......... would come round he would be able to get my body or bones, which I would like to have laid in Belvedere. If I had you, or at least if I were with you and my dear children, and had the clergyman, I don't think I should fear death half so much. I must now, my darling take my last farewell off you in this world. May we meet and enjoy one another where there is no sorrow, no trouble, no afflictions.

I leave you my love, my blessing.

Your loving but unfortunate husband
F. Dowsley

But Dr. Dowsley did not die so easily, and the following day penned another short letter to his wife.

Wednesday, Dec. 18, 1867

I have been out to see if there might be any chance of a rescue; but no such thing. I am almost mad with thirst. I would give all I ever saw for one drink of water, but I shall not get it. We are all wet and frozen. I am now going under the canvas to lie down and die. May God pity and have mercy on my soul!

However, Dr. Dowsley didn't die and on Christmas Eve, he penned what was to be his last sad letter to his wife and family.

Gull Island, off Cape John, Dec. 24th.

My Darling Margaret:
    We are still alive, and only that. We have had no relief ever since, nor any sign of it. We have not tasted a bit of food of any kind with the exception of the dirty snow water that melts around under our feet, which we are very glad to devour. The place we are sheltered in if I can call it a shelter is up to our ankles in water. What a sad Christmas Eve and Christmas Day it is for me! I think I can see you making the sweet bread and preparing everything comfortable for tomorrow. My feet were very painful last night. I was in complete agony with them. My clothes are completely saturated. I never knew how to appreciate the comforts of a home or a bed until now. If I were home, and to have you and the chil-

dren beside me, and have the clergyman, I think the trial would be small to what it is now; but we shall never see one another in this world. I had no idea we should have lasted so long. Our case is now hopeless; there is no hope for deliverance. My sufferings have been beyond description since I landed on this barren rock... How I dread — I would write more, but feel unable. My darling, if I could but once see you and the children I would be satisfied. Embrace them for me. {A few words of loving farewells to his family and a request for prayers follows, and he closes this last letter by signing himself}.

Your loving but unhappy husband
F. Dowsley

Then there was supposed to have been a notebook belonging to William Hoskins. Unfortunately, this notebook was lost or misplaced shortly after the discovery of the bodies. According to some contemporary writers who do not give the notebook entries a date, the entry was said to read: "We are starving and frozen and must draw lots so that some might keep alive longer should help come."

Then there is another line which says: "We have drawn, the lot fell to my poor sister. I have offered to take her place. The horror of it all!"

The terrible tragedy of the shipwrecked suffers on Gull Island touched the hearts of all Newfoundlanders, and the horrifying circumstances surrounding the wreck of the *Queen of Swansea* passed into the realm of folk legend.

On April 25, 1867, the Fortune Harbour correspondent of the St. John's paper the *Newfoundlander* wrote a letter telling of the details leading up to the discovery of the bodies on Gull Island. The report mentioned that it had been reported that lights had been seen on Gull Island, but no one bothered to investigate.

According to a local tradition in the area, it was a "simple boy" who used to walk at all hours about Shoe Cove that reported seeing the lights, but no one believed him. On Christmas Eve he again reported seeing lights, but no one bothered to go investigate. The Fortune Harbour correspondent ended his letter with the words, "It is a sad, sad history that will not soon be forgotten."

The remains of Felix Dowsley were brought to St. John's and buried in Belvedere cemetery as he had requested. There was such a public outcry after the disaster that the government had a small cabin built on the island. It was stocked with food so that another tragedy like that of the *Queen of Swansea* might be averted.

Strange to say, the cabin did prevent another tragedy some years later when a couple of men out birding swamped their boat and took refuge on Gull Island. After a couple of days with the food supply running out, the two men dismantled the cabin and used the wood to build a scow which got them to Shoe Cove.

Some years later a lighthouse was constructed on Gull Island and Captain Rowsell, who had discovered the bodies, was appointed lighthouse keeper, a position he held for many years. A monument was also erected on Gull Island to the memory of those who perished in the tragedy.

Sources

"Going Out in the Mummers or Jannies," previously unpublished article by Alice Lannon and Mike McCarthy.

"The Christmas Tree in Newfoundland Christmas Customs," previously unpublished article by Mike McCarthy.

"Hunting the Wren," by W.P., *Christmas Bells*, 1893.

"A Glimpse of Christmas in the Olden Times," by P.K. Devine, *Christmas Bells*, 1910.

"Quaint Christmas Customs," by P.K. Devine, *Christmas Bells*, December, 1901.

"Newfoundland Christmas Treats," by Alice Lannon, previously unpublished article.

"The Christmas Concert at St. Joseph's, St. Mary's Bay," by Joseph Dobbin, privately published as a Christmas Card in 2000.

"The Pathway To Yesterday," by John Maclay Byrnes, Boston, 1938.

"Brave Martin Lane," by Mrs. Anderson, *Christmas Bells*, 1900.

"A Christmas Miracle," by Mike McCarthy, previously published as the "Angel Priest."

"A Strange Christmas Box," by J. W. Kinsella, *Christmas Bells*, 1904.

"A Child's Christmas Prayer," by J.W. Foley, *Commercial Annual*, Christmas Number, December 1920.

"Nellie's Christmas," by Restrospect, *Daily Colonist*, Christmas Number, 1891.

"George Skinner's Christmas," by P.K.D., *Christmas Bells*, 1902.

"The Boy Who Almost Got Nothing for Christmas," by Alice Lannon, an oral family story.

"Christmas at St. Lewis Bay Trading Post, Labrador," by Lambert De Boilieu, *Recollections of Labrador Life*, London, 1861.

"How I Spent Christmas on the French Shore," by Reverend T.E. Lynch, *Daily Colonist*, Christmas Number, December, 1886.

"First Christmas at St. Thomas's Home, Villa Nova," by Father Michael Morris, *Evening Telegram*, Christmas Number, December, 1885.

"Memories of Christmas in an Outharbour," by Mary J. Lynch, *Daily Colonist*, Christmas Number, 1887.

"Christmas at Hopedale, Labrador," by Samuel King Hullon, *A Shepherd in the Snow*, London, 1893.

"Memories of Christmas," by John Maclay Byrne, *Trade Review*, Christmas Number, 1921.

"Christmas at King's Cove, Bonavista Bay," J.T. Lawton & P.K. Devine, *Old King's Cove*, St. John's, 1900.

"One Christmas in Germany," by Captain Leo Murphy, *Trade Review*, 1919.

"Memories of a Christmas Eve Long Ago," by Tim Shannahan, *Holly Leaves*, Christmas 1921.

"Christmas on the S.S. *Baccalieu*," by Alice Lannon, privately published for family members, 1999.

"Childhood Memories of a Christmas Eve in St. Joseph's, St. Mary's Bay," by Joseph Dobbin, privately published as a Christmas Card, 1988.

"A Fogo Island Christmas," by Mike McCarthy, *The Monitor*, Christmas Supplement, December, 1980.

"Christmas Night on the Cape Race Cliffs," by Frank Galgay & Mike McCarthy, *Shipwrecks Volume III*, St. John's, 1995.

"A Gull Island Christmas Tragedy," by Frank Galgay & Mike McCarthy, *Shipwrecks of Newfoundland & Labrador Volume 1*, St. John's, 1987.

Bibliography

BOOKS:

Anspach, Rev. Louis, *A History of Newfoundland*, London, 1827.

Bartlett, Captain Bob, *The Log of Bob Bartlett*, New York, 1928.

Boilieu, Lambert de, *Recollections of Labrador Life*, London, 1861.

Bonneycastle, Richard, Sir, *Newfoundland in 1842*, London, 1843.

Burke, Maurice, *Memories of Outport Life*, St. John's, 1985.

Byrnes, John Maclay, *The Paths to Yesterday*, Boston, 1931.

Devine & Lawton, *Old King's Cove*, St. John's, 1944.

Devine & O'Mara, *Noteable Events*, St. John's, 1900.

Fairford, Ford, *Peeps At Many Lands*, London, 1928.

Galgay & McCarthy, *A Christmas Box*, St. John's, 1988.

Halpert & Story, *Christmas Mummering in Newfoundland*, Toronto, 1969.

Hullon, Samuel King, *A Shepherd in the Snow*, London, 1938.

Maloney, Queen, *Trail Wanderings*, St. John's, 1994.

Pedley, Charles, Rev., *The History of Newfoundland*, London, 1863.

Prowse, D.W., K.C., *A History of Newfoundland*, London, 1895.

Ryan, D.W.S., *Christmas*, St. John's, 1988.

Sparkes R.F., *The Winds Sigh Softly*, St. John's, 1981.

Tizzard, Aubrey M., *On Sloping Ground*, St. John's, 1984.

MAGAZINES AND NEWSPAPERS:

Daily News, January 3, 1907.

Evening Telegram, Christmas Number, 1885.

Holly Leaves, December, 1917.

Christmas Bells, 1891, 1892, 1893, 1897, 1900, 1902, 1904, 1911, 1912, 1914, 1917.

Commercial Annual, Christmas Number, 1920.

Daily Colonist, Christmas Number, December 1891.

Newfoundlander, January 8, 1857, May 4, 1868.

Times, January 8, 1868.

Trade Review, Christmas Number, 1894, 1921.